Out of the Shadow

The Sequel to
In the Shadow of the Bayonet

Chris Boult

First published in Great Britain by Pen Press

All paper used in the printing of this book has been made from
wood grown in managed, sustainable forests.

ISBN13: 978-1-78003-789-9

Printed and bound in the UK
Pen Press is an imprint of
Indepenpress Publishing Limited
25 Eastern Place
Brighton
BN2 1GJ

A catalogue record of this book is available from
the British Library

Cover design by Jacqueline Abromeit

Dedicated to Esther Cairns

A much loved friend and colleague

Acknowledgements

I would like to thank all those who have helped to inform, advise and support me in this venture, especially those who have given their time to read passages, proof read drafts and make suggestions.

Thanks too to all who have helped promote the first book. For those who have read it, I hope you enjoyed it and look forward to concluding the story in the sequel.

Also to the publishers for their support and to all those people who I have worked with, both staff and offenders, over many years who have helped provide inspiration.

Glossary of Terms

Bang up	Lock up
Category A	Highest security prison for the most dangerous offenders
Category B	Next highest security prison on scale of 4 moving to less secure from A-D
Category C	Next security level where some opportunity starts to engage with the outside world
Category D	Open conditions with opportunities for low risk prisoners to work in the community.
CC	Confinement in cell as a punishment for offences dealt with in prison
CO	Commanding Officer
Closet Chain	Means by which to extend handcuffs to allow toileting
Cuffed up	Wearing handcuffs
DOP	Drop off point
Hooch	Prison slang for home-made illicit alcoholic drink
HR	Human resources
IRT	Immediate Response Team
MAPPA	Multi agency public protection arrangements
Numpty	Slang for idiot
OMU	Offender Management Unit
OM	Offender Manager
OS	Offender Supervisor

Parole Board An independent body that adjudicates on sentence progression and potential release of serious offenders.

Personal Officer

Prison officer assigned to take a specific interest in an individual prisoner

PUP Pick up point

Recce Reconnaissance, to check out, to survey a situation in advance

Risk Assessment

Process to define the likely risk an offender poses of reoffending and causing harm.

ROTL Release on temporary licence

RSM Regimental Sergeant Major

Seg Segregation unit

Sentence Planning

Process that sets targets for the offender to achieve aimed at reducing risk

Tariff Minimum term a life sentence prisoner must serve before consideration for release

The Clink A restaurant open to the public run by prisoners

TSP Thinking skills programme

Preface

The story continues from my first novel *In the shadow of the Bayonet*. It starts with Steve Mantel facing a life sentence and tells the story of that experience and beyond. It is self-contained so it is not essential to have read the first book, although you may think that it helps to set the context.

The characters in the story are entirely fictional and any resemblance to names of real life individuals is unintentional, for which I apologise in advance. Also the places and institutions, whilst based on reality, do not represent any particular real life settings, nor do any opinions expressed represent any official views from any of the criminal justice or government agencies involved.

In an attempt to maintain a reasonably realistic timescale, I have started when Steve was sentenced in 2013. Therefore release is projected into the future. I have taken the liberty of some speculation about how that future may look, but with some poetic licence. Any portrayal therefore of future events should not be taken too seriously.

Finally, I would like to take the opportunity to acknowledge the good work that is done by all concerned in Britain's prisons and indeed by those who take a wider view of justice and those who work in an international context.

PART ONE

Chapter 1

The cell door opened and Steve Mantel walked in to start his life sentence. It felt very strange. Thoughts took him back to the scene at the Sun Strip Bar, the stabbing, the bayonet and the injustice. He would never be a soldier again and it would be years until he could see former mates from the Parachute Regiment. The cell was small, but adequate, perversely far better equipped than his bed space in Camp Bastion in Afghanistan had been. He thought of his family, of initial training and selection, of war and of politics. He remembered mates who hadn't made it back and those that would never be the same.

Steve was about to enter a new world, one that was unfamiliar and one for which he was ill prepared. His uniform had changed to dull prison issue and his status from private soldier to prisoner, both, as it happened, with a number. He was however proud of one number and not the other. Not that he necessarily regretted the action that had brought him here; he regretted how it had turned out, but not his intention to expose a far more serious and dangerous 'criminal' than himself. That had been laudable and hanging on to that thought was important to him. Yes, a man had died, but another, Stefan Markou had escaped.

Steve Mantel had served with distinction in the British Army, but then had been convicted of the murder of a civilian in a Cypriot court and sentenced to life imprisonment, to be served in a UK jail. As an ex-soldier he was used to discipline, to order and routine and to being 'processed', but all of that in his past life was to serve a certain purpose. In this new context, although many of those features remained, their purpose was much more nebulous; to pass time, to punish, supposedly to rehabilitate. It had seemed like a long journey from Cyprus and he had arrived at HMP Ashcourt, a Category A, high security prison in England, where he had experienced initial reception. The staff he found were by and large firm but reasonable, given the context. In fact he couldn't help feel that this was in fact a military exercise, or indeed for real; that he had been captured and at any time now the punishment, interrogation and torture would start. He had been taught resistance to interrogation techniques and was trying to focus on the mental preparation to endure what was to come. Ironically, as he was to discover, in many ways this was to be a period of torture, but not short, violent and concentrated, but prolonged, slow and much more subtle. His ability to resist and to confront some demons was about to be tested to the full… and the journey would be a long one.

His sentence to life imprisonment included a tariff of ten years, the minimum term he must serve before any consideration of release on parole. Steve Mantel was now a lifer; a life sentence prisoner.

****

Anya Jabour was a lawyer working in Cyprus, who had defended Steve at his trial. She was a very strong minded woman and a formidable lawyer, but even her best efforts had brought little reward in this case. Steve Mantel had been lined up to be shot down and the authorities had their way. Anya took the long term view. She accepted that the world was not an entirely just place; prejudice, inequality and discrimination were still prevalent and things change slowly. She contented herself nevertheless that the struggle was worth it and to be satisfied with small but significant strides forward. In Steve's case, although she felt uncomfortable about the outcome, she accepted that for the foreseeable future there were no realistic grounds for appeal or intervention to argue to either overturn his conviction or reduce his length of sentence. He was where he was and that is how it is.

Rasha Ammar, now aged seventeen had a different perspective. She was not legally trained, although she had been working for Anya, learning English and practicing administrative skills. Her interest was more personal. Steve Mantel had bravely rescued her from a seedy brothel in Cyprus after her harrowing journey from Egypt. She had found herself to be a victim of the criminal gangs that prey on the desperate and extract money for services not rendered. Her family had thought they had invested in her future and secured her passage out of the chaos to safety, but they had been misled. She was earmarked for the personal attention of Stefan Markou, a prominent Cypriot businessman and politician as well as a ruthless criminal, specialising amongst other things in people trafficking. Steve had saved her from a life of misery and abuse and for that she would always be grateful. But there was more; for an aspiring young woman of only sixteen at the time, the event had represented something more significant. It had been her first experience of feelings of love towards a young man. Their contact had been so very brief, but she felt in her heart some sense of destiny and that she continued to feel drawn to this man despite his imprisonment. Anya had tried to place the event in some context for Rasha and gently point out the realities of her situation with Steve Mantel, now a life sentence prisoner in another country. Anya could see however that despite the situation rational argument was not going to overcome emotional attraction.

Chapter 2

'Mantel, come with me, you have an appointment at OMU,' ordered the prison officer gruffly.

Steve was happy to comply, both out of curiosity and an opportunity to break the boredom. An appointment to read the telephone directory would at least offer variety from the crushingly predictable and heavily controlled regime. After being searched before leaving the wing, Steve followed the officer obediently through locked gates and corridors to places in the prison he had not seen. All prisoner movement was escorted and often individually or in small groups. Movement was tightly controlled, ensuring a constant accurate picture of who was where, with checks before leaving the wing and again on arrival at the predetermined location. Searches, waiting and precise orders about even the simplest of tasks were already apparent to him as an integral part of his new life. It felt like he couldn't fart without notifying six people in advance, being observed doing it and having it recorded in multiple different information systems afterwards.

'This is OMU,' stated the officer to Steve, as they stood next to a large sign that read - Offender Management Unit. He checked his radio, searched Steve again and entered the unit, ordering him to sit and wait, before leaving and heading back to the wing.

Steve looked around at the new, clean institutional walls. HMP Ashcourt was one of the new generation prison buildings, built privately and leased back to the government. It was state of the art, with a mass of cameras and technology designed to ensure safety and control, with minimal staffing and thereby reduced cost. It was run by the public sector prison service. As he sat waiting, with no other prisoners within sight, he wondered what an OMU was and what it did. He almost felt some sense of excitement waiting to find out.

An officer appeared from behind a locked door, introduced himself and called him forward. After the customary search he was invited into an interview room.

'Mr Mantel, I'm Officer Wright. I work here in OMU. I've called you today for your induction.'

Officer Wright explained that OMU was a multi disciplinary team with prison officers, probation officers and psychologists. He continued that their role was to manage his sentence by completing a risk assessment and a sentence plan.

'One of the psychologists will then make a further assessment with you and work on analysing your offence.'

'You do realise I didn't do it, don't you? I didn't kill the man myself,' Steve replied.

'OK, but the court obviously decided differently. You will get your chance to explain your side of the story, but we are not here to establish your innocence; be clear about that from the start. We have to work on the assumption that the court got it right. If you sincerely believe that not to be the case, then the onus is on you to appeal, but simply trying to blank everything on the basis that you didn't do it ultimately won't help you.'

'Even if it's true?' responded Steve.

'But at this point in time it's not true. You have been convicted of murder, get that into your head,' was the stark but honest reply.

The officer completed some basic induction forms and gave Steve an outline idea of how his sentence was likely to progress. He explained that he was a category A prisoner, the highest security level, and would be managed under those conditions until the prison authorities were satisfied that he had made sufficient progress to move to a category B prison where the restrictions weren't quite so onerous.

'Fuck that!' responded Steve, 'I didn't fucking do it and you nor your fancy friends are not going to persuade me otherwise, so forget it. I do ten years for something I didn't do and then I walk, right?'

'Wrong, mate! No, it doesn't work like that. Ten years is your minimum term, but you won't be released until the Parole Board are satisfied that your risk has been sufficiently reduced to be manageable in the community. Then you will remain on life licence for life,' Officer Wright explained.

'Hey, wait a minute. No one explained that shit to me! You mean I'm literally trapped for life?' exclaimed Steve.

'Despite popular conception, a life sentence does mean life. Life, that is under supervision either in custody or in the community. I'm sure that would have been explained to you, but you are not unusual if you are saying that the whole court process is a blur. Welcome to reality!'

Steve was escorted back to his cell for lunch time bang up. He didn't think the food was too bad. It certainly wasn't bread and water or gruel! In fact he was surprised how accommodating the prison actually was in trying to service vegetarians, vegans and a plethora of religious requirements. It was a long way from sausage and beans in the soldier's canteen! The down side, of course, was being told what to eat and when to eat, with no flexibility to just go and make yourself a bit of toast or something, but it was prison after all. Steve was trying to adjust to the new routine and use his time constructively. He was determined not to vegetate and just switch off. He had enquired about education. He didn't get much out of school and this was at least a second chance to engage with formal education and get some qualifications. He was amazed at the range available, but some of the more experienced prisoners told him that there were complications and barriers to access. Also, this would be a very individual style of learning, basically self taught correspondence courses, but with time on his hands and modules that he could deal with at his own pace, this at least was a constructive opportunity. After some quiet reading, he was called again and taken back to OMU, he assumed for more 'processing.'

There he met his allocated probation officer, Kirsty Abbingdon, a bright, lively young woman, who he at least felt he could talk to. Kirsty introduced herself.

'Hi, Mr Mantel, I'm Kirsty Abbingdon. I shall be working with you in the prison. I work as your OS, offender supervisor and link with your outside probation officer in your home area, the OM, offender manager. Happy with first names, yes?' She took it from Steve's nod that he was. 'Steve I'm here to help you try to understand what you did, the impact on others and most importantly how to avoid doing anything similar again. Now you are subject to a life sentence, do you understand what being a lifer means?'

'Kirsty, I'm beginning to realise it means my life is no longer my own.'

'OK, that's one way of putting it. Yes, you will be subject to considerable controls and restrictions for years to come, but that is the response to murder, I make no apology for that. You have to understand that whatever the details of what happened, you are here with a chance to rehabilitate, but there are no second chances for the victim. The man died and he's not coming back. His family have to live with that. Hang on to that thought if you are tempted to feel sorry for yourself; just remember the victim.'

Steve pondered. She had a point.

'I'm new to all of this and used to a whole set of military jargon, so you'll have to give me a chance to mug up all the new terms. Just explain in simple terms again what you just said about what you do?'

'OK. Yes there will be lots of new jargon. Probation officers basically assess risk, the risk of you reoffending and the likely impact that may have. Then we identify areas of learning with you, monitor your progress and try to make it less likely that you will repeat such behaviour. Doing that helps to protect the public and helps you to rebuild your life. Does that make sense?' Kirsty tried to explain it as simply and succinctly as she could.

'Yeah, I think so. I've not been in prison before and not even been in court either. I've been close a couple of times as a kid, but I'm straight in here in the deep end. I don't want to go through this again!'

'Good. So let's start with the offence. Tell me simply what happened.'

Steve explained how he had got involved in identifying Stefan Markou as a people trafficker and that the authorities didn't seem to be doing anything about it. How he had observed some of his activities and how he felt it was wrong and that Markou should be challenged. Then how he and two of his mates had gone to Markou's bar and confronted him, resulting in one of Markou's men getting stabbed.

'What did you expect to happen when you confronted him? Did you plan to kill him?' she asked.

'It sounds daft, but I didn't really know. I was so angry I just wanted to expose him for what he was. I didn't think what would happen then, and no, I had no intention of killing anyone, although as it's turned out I might as well have killed Markou himself. I certainly wasn't after his mate and it was actually Markou who positioned my hand and tripped the guy over, to make sure we all fell on top of him,' Steve explained.

'So whose knife was it?'

'The bayonet?'

'Oh, was it a bayonet?'

'Yes, a British Army issue, but it wasn't mine as they said in court. It was Markou's mate's. He came at me with it and I disarmed him, as I'd been trained to do, and then picked it up. It was then that Markou grabbed my hand.'

'So are you saying Mr Markou deliberately positioned your hand to try to injure his own man?' queried Kirsty in disbelief.

'Right! And more than that, he must have wanted him to be killed!' Steve started to raise his voice.

'Why?'

'I guess coz he was getting me to do his dirty work, knowing people would believe him and I'd get the blame!' replied Steve, becoming emotional.

'OK, OK, calm down. I know this is difficult, but I just need to be clear what you say happened, then I can compare the details against the official account,' Kirsty said firmly, but calmly.

'So you can then call me a fucking liar!' exclaimed Steve, as he stood up.

One of the officers immediately entered the interview room on hearing raised voices.

'Mantel, final warning, wind it in or you're on report! You OK, Miss?'

'Yes, fine, thanks. I'm happy to carry on as long as you assure me Steve that you will try to stay calm.'

'Yes, yes, I'm sorry, Miss. Sorry Gov, lost it a bit; I'll calm it down. She'll be OK.'

As a Category A prison, HMP Ashcourt housed some very dangerous men, and staff were always alert to the potential for violence. Prisoners had to be confronted at times with the inconsistencies in their account and faced with the consequences of their actions, but always with suitable safeguards and control.

'Steve, you have to understand my role here. I'm not here to rerun your trial. The court have found you guilty, I take that as a given. What I'm trying to do, away from the pressure of the court hearing is establish in more detail what was going through your mind at the time and why you did what you did. OK?' said Kirsty regaining control.

'Yes, but whatever you say, I didn't kill the man; Markou did,' Steve said calmly with his eyes starting to moisten.

'Didn't it occur to you that in confronting Mr Markou things could turn violent?'

'Miss, I'd just come back from a fucking war! I'm a paratrooper! Violence is what I do! We weren't threatened by this guy and his mates. We knew we could handle ourselves... and before you ask, you may not believe me but we didn't go armed, not with weapons anyway, just ourselves. If that guy hadn't produced a knife... Yes, there was going to be blood. My mates took the two wingers out no problem, put 'em straight on the deck, and we may have roughed up Markou a bit, put him in his place, showed him he wasn't as untouchable as he thought...but we wouldn't have killed him,' Steve explained passionately but calmly, as the officer looked in through the observation glass again. There was a pause.

'I see,' responded Kirsty, 'but you have to accept that you did hold the knife and you did kill him. Didn't you?' she challenged him again, albeit with some trepidation about his likely reaction.

'Kirsty, I was holding the knife because I picked it up off the floor to prevent being attacked myself. But when someone else holds your arm and pulls you down on top of another guy, like a collapsing scrum, with your two mates pushing from behind and the weight of all that forces the knife deep into the mans chest, how is that my fault? How is that murder? You send me abroad in the Queen's name to kill terrorists, but when I challenge this bloke whose doing pretty much the same thing as the Taliban, I end up on a murder charge. I don't get it?' retorted Steve with tears now appearing on his cheeks.

In the days and weeks that followed, more interviews continued the process of exploring the details of events that night. Kirsty was challenging, and although Steve wondered if she had any understanding of what it is like to fight a war, he accepted that she was doing her job.

Kirsty had finished her initial assessment and had asked the officers to bring Steve across to OMU to discuss the results. On arrival Steve was mildly intrigued. He had not been subject to such scrutiny before.

'Steve, come in and sit down.' Kirsty was warm but professional. 'I've completed your assessment and sentence plan and wanted to go through it with you.'

'OK. What have you found? Am I mad?' Steve replied.

'No. I'm not a psychiatrist, but I don't think you are mad! Steve, firstly in terms of risk, the assessment indicates a low likelihood of further offending but a high risk of harm. That means, given your history at age twenty, with no previous convictions, statistically I would not expect you to be likely to reoffend, however if you were to reoffend, given your conviction, the consequences would be likely to be serious. Put simply, I don't think you'll do it again, but if you did you'd do it big time,' explained Kirsty trying hard to use language she thought Steve would relate to.

'OK. So does that mean I'll get out in ten years then?' responded Steve.

'No, it doesn't; too early to say, Steve. What we have to do is to be more specific and identify areas you need to work on, match those with interventions and monitor the outcome in order to assess their impact on risk.'

'And in English?'

'I'm sorry Steve. We need to find out what are the things about you that you need to change. Give some guidance, either talking to staff individually or in a group on courses, and see over time if you can adapt and manage those difficult areas better. OK so far?'

'Yes, I think I've got that.'

'Then if we can say that you have developed new skills in the way you deal with things and are using them effectively, then we could say to the Parole Board that risk has been reduced and you are better able to operate in the community without getting into trouble. That make sense?' Kirsty enquired.

'Um, all new to me, but I'm trying to grasp what you are getting at. So where do we start?' replied Steve.

'Right; I have identified some problem areas; anger, emotional control, decision making and consequential thinking to start with. We need to explore why you felt so angry, why you seemed unable to control your emotions and why you chose to deal with the situation in the way that you did, without thinking it through. To do that, you'll have some individual sessions with me and with one of the psychologists and I will refer you to some courses, including one called TSP. That is the bones of your sentence plan, OK? I'll print you off a copy of the full version to keep. As a lifer, start to get into the habit of keeping your own records. You will find that over time as you move prisons and deal with different staff that you need to be the continuity and the expert on your own case.'

'Um, more new tactics...there's going to be a lot of thinking here, I'm more used to action, I'm going to miss that!' responded Steve.

'Yes, you face a lot of adjustment, Steve. From the army to the prison is not the best preparation for life in the community, but that's what we've got and we have to deal with it.'

Steve appreciated Kirsty's attempts to be straight with him and to explain things. He was used to just being given orders: come here, go there, open fire, but here it was go away and think about this. Not the same thing at all.

Over time Kirsty talked through the areas she had identified, challenging him and starting him thinking. He also saw the psychologist, Lucy Grove, whom he readily grew to like.

Chapter 3

Lucy Grove read through Steve's case file. She quickly got the picture. She would make her own assessment to complement Kirsty's, but from the file read she agreed on the areas Kirsty had identified. She was waiting to meet him.

Steve was escorted through to OMU on what had become a familiar journey.

'Good morning; Steve isn't it?' she held out her hand to meet him. He took it firmly and responded with a powerful hand shake. 'OK, no need to pull my hand off! Right, I've read your papers and spoken to Kirsty and now need to go through a few things with you. OK?'

'Fire away,' responded Steve, quizzing her appearance.

'I'm Lucy Grove, one of the psychologists. We work closely with probation here. We look at things from a different angle and that makes assessment a stronger process. You will find during your sentence that you seem to continually repeat things. Different staff will ask similar questions over time, and what we look for is consistency and some positive change. The areas I'd like to discuss with you are; anger, emotional control, decision making and obsession. Today I want to start with anger. So Steve can you just tell me in your own words what you think makes you angry?'

'Being asked the same daft questions by people like you,' Steve responded.

'OK, if you want to be flippant, I can send you back to the wing and you'll move to the back of the queue, if that's what you want?' Lucy replied confidently.

'I'm sorry, Miss. I'm just not used to this. Kirsty went on about all of this. I don't think I'm an angry person. You have to understand that paratroopers need to be aggressive and I was encouraged and trained that way,' Steve responded.

'Yes, I can see that; I've dealt with ex-soldiers before. Surely you are also taught to control that aggression?'

'Yes, I suppose so, but life in a parachute battalion, particularly when at war is all pretty aggressive.'

'Yes, I expect so, and you are not unusual in struggling to adjust from acceptable behaviour in one environment to another. If you had met your victim on the battlefield and he came at you with a bayonet, you would presumably have been expected to kill him without question? But of course you didn't and the same rules don't apply.'

'Yes, I hadn't thought of it like that. In my mind I didn't think I was still on the battlefield and I didn't intent to kill anyone, nor did I need to kill him to defend myself,' Steve explained.

'So accepting you were operating in a civilian environment, why did you feel so angry that you felt it was your role to investigate and confront this local dignitary?' she challenged.

'Coz he was a slimy shit and no fucker else was doing it!' exclaimed Steve.

Steve explained more about what he knew of Markou's activities, the rumours of involvement in illegal immigration, his own observations during the recce on the beach watching him receive desperate people off a small boat, the chaos of the shipwreck and the rescue of the small boy, his rescue of Rasha from the brothel and his memories of his Syrian grandmother that all led to his growing anger at injustice. How could the authorities ignore what was so plainly in front of them and do nothing? Having seen some of his mates die trying to stop this sort of thing in Afghanistan, how could it be allowed to happen in Cyprus?

Lucy continued, 'Steve, you make some good points there but it seems to me that there are three issues here. Accepting there is something in the inconsistency of morality being applied in what you describe: firstly, was it your role to intervene? Secondly do you think you let your emotions take control? And thirdly do you think your decision making was poor in responding to those feelings? Just think about those questions. They are quite challenging. Don't be afraid to be self critical. I want you to think about it seriously and then we can discuss it next time, OK?'

'I'm not sure I'm going to be very good at this,' Steve responded. 'I'm not used to this kind of thing; I'm not entirely sure I get it.'

'Don't worry, just have a go. Then later I can give you some help in improving your understanding, but for now I just need to establish a starting point, where you are with this. It's not a test. There are no right or wrong answers. I just want to get an idea of how you think.'

Steve left feeling a little confused and more inclined to concentrate on remembering the passing view of Lucy's cleavage than what she said. The officer led him back to the wing.

'How was that then Mantel?' he asked.

'The session? Yes OK, but it's all a bit heavy; I'm just not used to this.'

'Yeah, I think they can forget that we don't all use all those long words and stuff, but I do see the penny drop for some guys.'

Steve was due in education later, then work in the afternoon. He'd been allocated to gardens, which at least meant working outside and getting some exercise, which he was pleased about. The instructor was OK and they had been digging a vegetable plot, helping build a chicken pen and erecting a small fence, so it had been reasonable work and a good way of taking your mind off things.

When Steve returned for the next appointment he didn't know quite what to expect.

'So Steve, lets just recap and then I want to hear from you how you have got on thinking about those questions. I was trying to start you thinking about what you did and why, and asking could you have acted differently? So, was it your role to intervene?' Lucy asked.

Steve could accept that it wasn't but was still hung up on his perception that nobody was doing anything. Lucy encouraged him to think wider; would he necessarily know what the authorities were doing? Could he have been wrong and there was activity going on behind the scenes? Could he have helped them in any way? Had he tried to report his concerns officially? Lucy was trying to help Steve think more calmly and rationally and be less emotional and impulsive. He was struggling initially. Lucy led him through some simple exercises and set him some reading and cell work for next time.

This became the pattern over several months of one-to-one intervention; help with recognising his thinking style and input to help develop it into being more considered and less impulsive. Lucy understood that a military background encouraged action rather than deliberation. It would be no good, for example, as a response to coming under fire to break off into small groups and discuss the possible implications! Then form a committee and go away to deliberate or set off to research how such issues have been dealt with in the past and how effective those approaches had been. But meeting fire with fire wasn't always the best approach in a civilian context and certainly not the only one.

As they worked together, Lucy complemented Steve on his commitment to their sessions. It was true that although hard work, Steve was getting something out of his time with Lucy and was genuinely trying to understand what she was getting at. There was however a far simpler explanation. The fascination with how close her nipples were to the material of her blouse, a glimpse of cleavage, a view of how tight her trousers were if she got up from the desk before he did, a sniff of perfume, a smile. Was it so surprising that a young man in prison enjoyed what little opportunity he had to engage in female company? However, over time he did develop a growing respect for her as a person and as an official, but he couldn't help feeling drawn to her as a woman.

Chapter 4

The following day in a quiet corner during association Mantel was approached by a really big guy. Steve had met and worked with some very fit, capable and strong men, but this was something else. Some of these guys were massive. He was amongst gangsters, murderers, rapists, child abusers, drug dealers and terrorists to name but some. He was learning that prison culture dictated you were best to largely keep yourself to yourself and of course no one goes around with 'sex offender' or 'murderer' written on their head, so you are left guessing who is who and who has done what. The man made him a proposition.

'Mantel, I need a fighter, and I see you have anger in your eyes, so I want you. See that guy over there, the one talking to the officer by the pool table? Well, he doesn't know that we know, but he's a sex offender, a fucking nonce, he does kids, you know what I mean? Well he needs a kicking and I'm giving you the job.'

'And if I refuse?'

'You don't refuse... This will help you, know what I mean? I know people who know people and that, see?'

No, Steve didn't see, but looking around, this big guy had eye contact with several other guys of a similar stature, so he thought he got the message, and why worry about a child molester anyway?

The plan was to distract the officer while the target was on cleaning duty. The big guys had worked out where there was a gap in the camera's field of view and that for potentially twenty seconds or so they could leave this creature with Mantel undetected. They waited and bided their time until the right combination of factors were all in place together; the right corner, the right target suitably isolated, Mantel's legitimate placement on the wing and the most susceptible officer on duty.

When Steve got the signal he grabbed the target, pushing him heavily into the wall. For what seemed like minutes he let loose a whole package of built up anger, pounding the guy with blow after blow, giving him no chance to react. At that moment Steve had no feeling for his victim, just a sense of relief in being able to release so much venom at one time. Again, at the given signal he moved away, leaving the target to fall to the floor. He had time to disperse before the reaction came with staff running from everywhere to deal with the situation. All the prisoners on the wing just looked blank in disinterest. No one saw anything. No one knew anything...and no one got caught.

After the event, Steve did think about what he'd done. The guy hadn't come back and was presumably in hospital. He didn't feel guilty directly about the guy. He could readily adopt a military rationale in distancing himself in these circumstances and not dwelling on the consequences. However, he could see that once again perhaps he had allowed himself to act instinctively and not thought it through. What would have happened if he had been caught? He had learnt enough to know that none of the other guys would say anything and just let him take the rap without a moment's hesitation. He also suspected that the prison authorities would conclude that this confirmed he was just 'a bad apple' and punish him even more. He didn't know what form that might take or realise just how far such an action could delay any consideration for release later. He accepted that this time he had been unwise and that he had been lucky.

****

Prison life continued with its crushing tedium and routine, it's ever present control and rules and regulations. He wondered what made people want to be a prison officer, particularly the young ones. Who would want to spend their working life in one of these places? He couldn't understand it. Small gestures and events helped to make things tolerable; a shared joke, any letters, phone calls to his mum, comfort food bought from his meagre prison wages. He was learning to block out the pain and regret and just live day to day and try not to think about how long all this would take.

Chapter 5

A week or so later Jason walked into his cell and started a conversation while offering Steve a fag.

'That's kind of you mate, but I don't smoke.'

'My body is a temple and all that crap?'

'No, I'm a soldier...an ex-soldier. Fitness is important to me.'

'What were you in mate?'

'The Para's, the best.'

'Try telling that to a Marine!'

'Why, were you a Green Beret?'

'No. Not my style mate. I was into gangs very young; quite heavy shit like, you know? Anyway, you want anything, just see me eh mate? I'll see you right,' said Jason as he left.

After he'd left Steve noticed a small package on his shelf. What's that he thought? The guy must have left it. Steve went out of his cell to find him, but Jason had gone. Steve didn't think anything of it and put the package away safe to catch up with him tomorrow. He had started reading anything he could get his hands on. He was reading a book from the library on the history of the Parachute Regiment. He didn't know half this stuff. It was at least a chance to use the time. In his cell at night Steve routinely completed an exercise routine in the limited space. He wanted to keep fit and access to the gym was limited. Most of the prisoners wanted to pump iron, he liked weights, but was used to running and he couldn't really do that in a cell so had to content himself with sit ups and press ups. It was better than masturbation.

The following day in the breakfast queue he saw Jason and approached him.

'Jason, morning. You left something in my cell yesterday. I'll bring it back to you later.'

'No mate, that's for you. A little something to help get through.'

'What! I don't do that shit!' Steve replied angrily.

'Hey, shhh, walls have ears, sssshhhhh.'

They eat their breakfast.

'You recruit that dude Jas?' asked Marvin in passing.

'Yeah, cool brother, he's with us now.'

Steve had a gym session next and was looking forward to it. The gym was an accepted means of relieving tension and keeping guys occupied. Steve was up for anything going. He had heard there was a rugby team. After the gym he got back to his cell and thought again about the package. He was new to all this but reckoned if it was drugs of some sort he was best off without it and certainly didn't want to be caught with it, so he flushed it down the toilet, thinking, there you go, that's the end of that!

The following day in the exercise yard, Jason approached Steve with Marvin.

'Steve, you had some stuff from my friend here, so you owes, you understand?'

'No. I didn't ask for it. I didn't want it.'

'Oh you didn't need to ask for it or want it boy. You just had it, so you owes. Later Jas will give you something. You just hold it for us.'

'Bollocks! You hold your own stuff,' replied Steve.

'Hey baby boy, now that really ain't wise. You are with us now and this is the price. Think about it.'

Marvin moved away as an officer was watching. Then it happened, in the opposite corner another prisoner went down like a coconut off a stand and hit the floor. Boots went in from all angles, alarm bells rang out. Staff started running. Steve, like the rest of the observers, was quickly guided back to his cell while order was restored. Cell doors were locked, numbers were accounted for and then the searching started. Steve could hear staff shouting and cell doors being opened quickly. He wasn't sure what was going on, but guessed they were looking for something. He was glad the small package had gone and indeed it was too early to be holding whatever Marvin had in mind for him. Steve was learning. There are times when you just have to let it all happen round you and there is nothing you can do about it. Whatever was scheduled for the afternoon would be cancelled and time in cell would be extended. Back to his books and his press ups.

By the next day, numbers on the wing were noticeably reduced. Marvin and Jason, to mention just two, were obviously absent. Nothing was said. Steve had learnt that prisoners come and go. Virtually no one gets released from Cat A so when people are gone they are either in the Seg or had been transferred. Constant movement seemed to be a method to break up trouble. His personal officer enquired if he was OK.

'Yes, what happened then?'

'Just prison life, Mantel, just prison life, that's how it is. They come and they go. Just remember there are no friends here. Most of these shits are just out for themselves; it's not like you're used to with real mates who would fight for each other, even die for each other; here they would sell their own grandmother,' Officer Carter explained.

Steve reflected; he would need to keep wising up if he was going to avoid trouble. He was learning fast.

Chapter 6

Letters were so important, even more so than in the army. At least there you always knew training or operations were time limited, but here time was open-ended and it dragged. Out of the blue, Steve had received a letter from his old CO, Lieutenant Colonel Lance Percy. He said that he had left the army and had set up his own business in adventure training. He had offered to come to visit Steve. He was touched and very pleased to send his old CO a visiting order. He remembered their last meeting when the CO had said he would probably never see him again. That was just before the RSM had chewed his balls off for letting down the battalion.

He also received regular letters from Rasha, occasionally from Anya and from his family. His dad didn't bother much, but Mum tried to keep in touch and support her son. Anya reported that there were no legal grounds for appeal against his sentence and that whilst she would endeavour to keep in touch there was little that she could do to help at present. Appeal against conviction was much more complicated and would take time, if it happened at all, unless something significant changed. She also said that she was thinking of moving to England and that she had applied to adopt the little boy that he had saved from the sea.

Rasha was obviously learning English well and her letters became more detailed over the next few months. She explained how she was working with Anya and learning all the time. Steve always felt that there was a warmth in her letters. It was not so much what she said or didn't say, but he could feel something when reading them, when just holding them. She was trying to communicate something else.

His mother's letters just talked of family and life at home. He remembered receiving similar ones when in Afghanistan. She was obviously disappointed about her son, but mainly she was just sad. His dad had been made redundant and things were quite tight at home. Mum was doing a few extra hours and they had cut back on a few things. She apologised that she couldn't help him more. Steve felt quite embarrassed that his mother was still trying to support him, but knew with his little legitimate earning power in prison any help from family or friends towards buying things like phone cards, stamps and just basic toiletries was always welcome.

After a second letter from his ex-CO explaining that he was still trying to keep Steve's name alive in Regimental circles, he was due to visit. A previous visit had been cancelled due to prison security concerns that day, so Steve was particularly looking forward to a visit that connected him with his old life. A private soldier had little direct contact with someone as high ranking as his CO and would normally only see him when saluting smartly or when being marched into his office for a bollocking under the watchful eye of his RSM. So this was unusual, and Steve was grateful that Colonel Percy had taken the trouble to stay in touch, especially as he had now left the army. He supposed that said something about the bond that remains between soldiers.

Lance Percy had been affected by the events in Cyprus, too. The Brigadier had not been impressed with his actions and the CO had read between the lines and concluded that this effectively meant career over for him, so with some reluctance he had decided to leave the army and make a new start on his own. He also felt let down by an institution he had always respected and admired that didn't deliver the loyalty that he would have expected. So this was a new opportunity. He had always been keen on adventure training and with his experience felt he could offer guided packages to the adventurous in places all over the world. In this context however, he could have been forgiven for taking the view that Steve Mantel and his two mates were to blame for ruining his career and not wanting to cast eyes on any of them ever again, but he didn't. As Steve had thought, the military bond goes deeper than that. Sure, Mantel had cocked things up in Cyprus big time and the negative consequences had been far greater than he could have anticipated with the political backlash, the cancellation of the Royal visit and the impact on military/civil relations. Mantel however was not wholly responsible for all of that, at least that was how the CO felt, and as such he still deserved some support. He remembered that Mantel had fought bravely in Afghanistan and was well thought of and would probably have done well in the army, had he stayed.

The visits room was relatively small and only small numbers of prisoners were facilitated visits at any one time. Movement in and out of prison is always a potential security threat and an opportunity to bring in or take out contraband or other risky items. Cash, drugs and mobile phone parts were the most popular items to target, if a prisoner attempts to 'persuade' a visitor to bring things in. As such, security was very tight in visits. All visitors went through a search process including an airport style metal detector check and were individually questioned about their knowledge of their responsibilities. If caught smuggling, penalties were harsh. No one could say they hadn't been warned. Not that the CO posed any threat to security.

As it was still early in his sentence prisoner Mantel was still assigned to closed visits; that is to sit opposite their visitor on bolted down chairs, but separated by a glass screen so there is no physical contact or opportunity to smuggle. Steve could live with that in this instant. He just wanted to earn enough trust to be allowed open visits when his family came.

Steve sat waiting in his allotted cubical. Eventually he saw the tall imposing figure of his CO arrive. Although he had said that he had left the army, Steve still saw him as his CO. He stood up and felt a little awkward as he waited to salute but realised that it would be inappropriate. The ex-CO smiled, as if he understood. Conversation was a little stilted through the glass screen, but they made the best of it.

'So, how have you been Steve?' Lance Percy asked.

'OK, Sir, on the whole,' Steve Mantel replied. 'Conditions aren't too bad, apart from being locked in. I really miss my mates and the army, but am trying to put that behind me and get on with it.'

'Wise man; I think that's all you can do.'

They talked about old times and Steve explained more about how his sentence was working out. The CO sounded genuinely interested.

'Did I fuck it up for you Sir, is that why you left the army?' Steve enquired.

'It certainly didn't help, but no, there were other reasons,' Lance replied kindly. 'Listen Steve, part of me feels bad about what happened to you. Your two mates will do alright I'm sure, they will carry on, but you really got hammered. I want you to understand that I really regret what happened, I don't condone it; that is, what you did or how the authorities reacted, but I think you were something of a scapegoat. I can't change that, although I wish I

45

could, but rest assured that I will do all I can to keep your cause alive in army circles and exert whatever influence I can to help you through this. You never know, if my new business goes well, I may even to able to offer you a job on release!'

Steve was surprised by the affection in the tone of what his CO had just said. He was also grateful and reassured. Being a prisoner, he was beginning to realise can be a very lonely place to be, but to know you have someone fighting on your side meant a lot. They continued to talk about the Regiment, Afghanistan and old stories until an officer called time and the CO was politely escorted out of the prison. Lance was glad that he had made the effort to visit...and so was Steve Mantel.

Chapter 7

Into his second year of sentence Steve received some good news from Anya and Rasha. Anya wrote explaining that she had secured a job in the UK, dealing particularly with immigration issues and foreign nationals, with a law firm in Manchester. The job was due to start in several months time, subject to checks and papers being correct. Anya sounded excited about the prospect, with a new start and being able to leave some of the bad feelings from the past behind. It would be a busy period with winding up her affairs in Cyprus. Also she had explained that she planned that Rasha would come too, as her assistant. There maybe issues with work permits/visas and so on, but Anya sounded confident that she could deal with all that.

Steve didn't know quite what to think. It would obviously be helpful in the future to have his lawyer available in the UK, but surely they were not moving just to accommodate him? Also there was Rasha; she would now be eighteen years old. Steve really didn't know how he felt about her now, or how he would react if he was to see her again? It had been a while and their contact had been so brief. He recognised that she had feelings for him, but wasn't sure whether this was just a passing crush; he didn't know. He felt that he couldn't talk to anyone in the prison about this, no one would really understand.

His next letter was from Rasha and her English was progressing. She rather assumed that in coming to the UK, she could visit him. He wasn't sure. Not only whether the authorities would allow it, but whether he really wanted it? Her letters weren't over the top, but he sensed that they carried much more affection than was expressed. How would he handle this, he thought … as a lifer?

It troubled him and the following week he saw a notice on the wing about the multi faith centre and on impulse asked if he could speak to one of the ministers. Steve wasn't really religious, only when he thought that he could be killed in Afghanistan had he really given any thought to these sorts of things. The staff representing different religions seemed to work as a team and one of them would walk the wings regularly, just talking to prisoners, listening to their concerns and trying, he supposed, to help keep a sense of calm. When the opportunity came, he took it and asked the Church of England minister if he could have a word. The man readily led him to a quiet room.

'How can I help you, my friend?' he asked gently.

'This is difficult; I'm only just turned twenty one and now a lifer; I'm not used to this game and there's a girl...' Steve started to explain.

'Ah, affairs of the heart, second only to complaints about the food, in my experience!' he interjected with a smile.

Steve smiled back and relaxed a little. 'Basically I rescued this girl from a brothel abroad and she's now working assisting my lawyer. She writes to me and I think she thinks she loves me and I'm not sure what to do?'

'An unconventional first date,' the minister commented, 'but follow your heart my son, that's all you can do. That's my best advice. You are wondering whether to stay in touch or let her go, is that it? Are you likely to see her?'

'Possibly, she is planning on moving to England and could then visit.'

'Then wait until you see her, then you'll know.'

****

Anya was very busy. She hadn't realised just how many contacts she had made whilst in Cyprus. She was pleased that she had managed to hand over some cases by recommending alternative lawyers to her clients, but nevertheless there would be loose ends. She had also met Mike, the ex-police DCI in town and he had mentioned the existence of a tape of the incident. This was exciting. If such evidence still existed, it was a significant development and may help Steve clear his name. She couldn't wait to tell him. Matters with her relocation were moving fast and she wanted to share that with him, too.

Steve eagerly opened his letter, recognising the writing and the post mark that it was from Anya in Cyprus. She started with some local Cypriot news and talked about her business and her move, then it hit him....HOPE! Anya said she had discovered that there was a CCTV tape running at the time of the incident leading to Markou's henchman's death, that she understood it was still in existence and that it demonstrated that the evidence against him was inconclusive! Steve's heart pumped and his mind started racing. Does this mean they will let me out? he thought. He danced around his cell, did twenty press ups and looked out of his barred window longing for the outside world. He felt he had done pretty well in not losing it so far and in dealing with his sentence and all that it meant, but now there was a chance of setting the record straight and returning to his previous life even. He wondered if that chance of promotion would still be available. Fancy that, he'd jump at the chance - Lance Corporal Mantel!

Steve eagerly eat his breakfast and waited in anticipation of unlock. Who could he tell? When would he pack his kit? What about transport? Where were the battalion now? All these questions were rushing through his head.

The cell door opened and the officer looked in to check that Mantel was present and alive then moved on with a cursory grunt. Steve shot out of the cell and seeing the first other prisoner exclaimed, 'I'm getting out! I'm getting out!'

The man barely looked up and just muttered, 'Oh yeah, aren't we all; aren't we all.'

'No *really*,' he emphasised. 'I've had a letter from my solicitor!'

'Tell that to half the landing, mate; some of us have been waiting for twenty years!'

Steve recoiled to get a grip of himself. It can't be that simple...

Steve returned to his cell to think again. Later the prisoner looked in on Steve sitting in the corner of his cell, staring into the abyss with eyes glowing red. 'If it's disappointment, mate, better get used to it, there'll be plenty more to come,' he advised and moved on.

Steve had picked up the letter again. He had jumped up at the first message initially but had failed to read on. The rest was far more sobering. The letter went on to say that although it seemed pretty clear that there was a tape, there was no guarantee that it still existed, that she could find it or be allowed to see it. Even if she could, if, as advised it proved to be inconclusive, the best he could hope for was not to prove his innocence but to cast some doubt on his guilt. Even then the evidence of the bayonet against him was much more powerful. She had explained the picture in detail and concluded with harsh reality '...So don't get your hopes up, this is an important development, but only a small step along what is likely to be a long road.'

Steve was gutted. He had allowed himself to ignite a glimmer of hope, only to see it fade and die so quickly. Maybe the other prisoner was right and indeed the psychologist. He was too emotional and not good enough at controlling it. It was hard, he thought, all my military training was geared towards being absolutely alert and reacting instantly to situations, sometimes without even a thought. We weren't there to think or to analyse, just to do. In this world however everything seems slowed down as if it demands thought and consideration before any kind of response. This was alien to him, but he was starting to get the message.

****

Later that year Steve was allocated a place on TSP, a thinking skills course. He was sceptical, but was told it was a requirement as it was on his sentence plan. To start with he just went through the motions, paying it lip service and adopting the tactic of telling the tutors what he thought they wanted to hear, but after a while he began to get into it. The course gave ample opportunity to practice and develop a more reflective and considered approach to decision making and life in general. There were role plays and both group and individual discussions, with a central message of 'Stop and Think'. Steve could see from the group discussions the tendency of members to just do it and not to think about it. One guy said he had just gone along with a loosely connected group of guys he used to hang about with and one day got into a car that he could see had shotguns on the floor. He didn't ask and nobody said, so he had just carried on. Then the other guys suddenly started putting masks on and told him to play look-out, be ready to drive and to use his mobile phone if there was a problem. The others got out and ran into a factory, some shots were fired and they ran out again carrying several large cash boxes and jumped into the car shouting, 'Drive! Drive!'

By the time he had gathered his breath and asked where to, they had gone round a corner straight into a police road block and were all caught red handed. As a result he got fifteen years for armed robbery along with the others, although he maintained he had no idea about what was going on. The point being that he hadn't stopped to think it through; if I go with these guys and they have weapons, what is likely to happen? What might be the consequences? And so on. That was the point of the course.

Over time with TSP and one to one work with both the probation officer and the psychologist, Steve was starting to realise that he was at least partly culpable and could have acted differently, which could have avoided the killing. He still felt that he was right to be concerned about the situation in Cyprus; the people trafficking and the abuse by people who Steve felt should have known better and by the fact that no one was doing anything about it. He had begun to accept however that it wasn't up to him to start a one man crusade. He felt he was learning and there was some comfort in that.

****

A year on and Steve was making steady progress. He felt that he had adjusted on the whole to prison life and was doing OK with his sentence plan. He had heard from Anya that her job had fallen through after complications about her and Rasha emigrating from Cyprus to the UK, but now that those obstacles were clear she wrote telling him that she had secured a new job opportunity in London. Suddenly everything was back on and there was a real urgency in getting all the practicalities sorted out.

The letter concluded that in order to confirm accommodation plans and arrangements for the new job, she and Rasha were going to visit London for several weeks next month and that they would be available to visit him in prison. Steve felt so excited, tempered by some misgivings: whether the authorities would approve the visit, but thinking about it Anya was his lawyer after all, and Rasha her assistant, so that was the way to approach getting approval. He was learning. Immediately he applied for authorisation for the visit and hoped that it would be approved without too many questions.

In the event, the prison authorities granted permission for Anya to visit, but not Rasha. This was a real disappointment, despite his mixed feelings. He wrote to Rasha and tried to explain to her how the rules applied. Steve was disappointed but could understand and was really looking forward to at least seeing Anya. He hoped that Rasha would be allowed to visit once they had moved to UK.

****

On receipt of the letter Rasha cried. Anya had anticipated that this might be the response so had tried to prepare her, but her efforts had fallen on deaf ears. She did feel really sorry for Rasha.

'Why do they have to make it so difficult!' Rasha shouted, stamping her feet and banging her fists. 'First they take him away and now when I find a way to follow him, they won't let me see him. I so desperately want to see him again, Anya,' she said as she sobbed. 'Anya, I know I only spent such a short time with him, but I love him Anya, I love him; you do know that don't you?'

'Yes Rasha, I knew it from the moment I first saw you with him. Love can endure Rasha; love can cross boundaries and love can prevail. Be patient Rasha, you will get to see him, I promise.'

'Oh Anya, I do hope so soon, my thoughts are with him, but I just want to be with him and I know he wants to be with me, too.'

'Rasha, I do urge you to be realistic. Steve faces at least another seven years in prison, so even if he does feel the same as you, it's still an awful long time to wait and to keep things going. I really hope that it all works out for you, but you can't guarantee it and you shouldn't put your life on hold while you wait.'

'What do you mean? I'm confused; you say those nice and reassuring things - that love can prevail - and then you tell me that it's not going to happen! What do you mean Anya?' Rasha cried out with tears running down her cheeks.

'Rasha, I believe in love and to some extent in destiny, but I'm just trying to temper that with an understanding of the difficulties that you both face. Rasha, please don't think I'm saying forget him, because I'm not, but live your life as well,' Anya responded trying so hard to be supportive but realistic.

'I can't! I just can't! Apart from you, he's all I have in the world and I can't let him go!' Rasha cried as she ran upstairs in tears.

Chapter 8

Over the following few months things moved quite quickly compared to the usual drudge of prison life. For Anya and Rasha, their move was all organised with the prospect of a new rented flat, new jobs in a good legal firm for both of them and Anya had resolved all matters about immigration for them both.

Steve had done well in HMP Ashcourt and was now considered safe to move on to Category B; that being the next step along the path from maximum security to release. In their correspondence they agreed that it would be sensible to wait until he had moved to a new prison before applying for visits. That would also give Anya and Rasha some time to settle into their new surroundings. Although Rasha in particular was desperate to visit Steve she could see the sense of what they had agreed, despite part of her feeling that this was yet another obstacle that had appeared to thwart her plans.

Prison moves usually take some time to organise and can change depending on security considerations. Prisoners aren't necessarily told final arrangements until the day of the move. That proved to be the case for Steve, not that he represented any great threat to security, but that a move had fallen through for another prisoner at the last minute and he was the next in the queue and had picked up the place. In fact Steve had only just asked Kirsty, Lucy and Officer Carter when he was likely to move and had been told to be patient, when the following day two officers unlocked in the morning and told him to pack his kit for a move in an hour.

With virtually no time to say goodbye, it was an odd feeling leaving his imposed home with a few meagre possessions to move to somewhere new and unfamiliar. Steve had of course done this many times in his army career, but always with his mates; this time he was on his own. He went through the security checks and signed the various papers before getting in the prison van. All he knew was that he was heading for HMP Farm Hill. He didn't know if it was north or south, or anything about it. Oh well, he thought, take it as it comes. All prisons are more or less the same.

The journey was long and north-bound judging by the traffic signs. It was dark by the time he arrived at what looked like a very new building. Some of the signage was different, with a company logo. A private prison, he thought. The van went through the usual security checks and sat in the compound for some time. The door then opened and Steve was invited out to follow the signs leading to reception where all the kit that had just been searched was searched again, despite being transported in a sealed cubicle. The place was obviously new and the staff wore different uniforms with the company logo for TS Securities.

'OK, Mr Mantel, I need to check a few details,' announced the officer

'Steven Mantel, subject to life, transferred from Ashcourt, first time in Cat B, is that correct?'

'Yes Sir,' replied Steve crisply.

'I'm sure Ashcourt prepared you for this move and briefed you about our facilities here, so as soon as we get your property booked in we'll get you allocated to a cell. You'll need to keep some clothes, there's no prisoner uniform here.'

'Actually, this was a sudden move. I know nothing about Farm Hill.'

'Oh well, you'll soon learn. This is a new private Cat B jail, only been open six months. We are still filling to capacity and looking to attract lifers. There is a lifer wing at present. We have state of the art education and workshop facilities, a good probation department who are offender supervisors for lifers. The gym has just opened and the gardens department which will grow all our own plants and some fresh food.'

Sounds like a recruitment drive, thought Steve, chuckling to himself. I'm not actually buying a cell space you know! Ashcourt was an austere old traditional public prison, so this was going to be a change.

When called he followed the officer to A wing; there were noticeably less locks, gates and the like on the way. The courtyard was modern, not like an old military fort, with open space, trees and even some benches, it actually looked almost inviting. A Wing was on House 1 which was a spur design with a central control room with wings running off in different directions. It was clean and tidy with a traditional landing and net, the inevitable pool table, a bank of phones and what looked like a laundry and a cafeteria style servery. The officer left him with his kit as he talked to the wing officer on duty, a young woman. Steve looked around and couldn't see any other members of staff. Several prisoners were wandering around and the officer shouted over to one prisoner to come and introduce himself and show Steve round.

'Hi, I'm Pedro. We are all lifers here, so it's pretty relaxed, we just sort things out ourselves and get on with it. The staff are mostly new and young, with fuck all experience. They pay them crap money so you can imagine what we get, but most are OK, as long as they listen to our advice. There are 60 lifers on this wing so far with space for 120. We must have over 500 year's prison experience between us, so we know the form. It's not a bad place.'

Steve was intrigued. He couldn't believe it - what a contrast!

'Mr Mantel, you're in cell 15, just down here. Follow me.'

'Mr' was a change! The cell was fine, reasonably clean with all plastic units, a sink, toilet and a shower! Steve dropped his kit and took stock. The officer gave him a breakfast pack for the morning, said a few words and locked the cell door. It was too dark to see anything from the window and although still quite early it seemed like a good opportunity to catch up on some kip, so he made up his bed and put his head down.

In the morning there was the usual induction, with explanation of local rules and expectations.

Pedro appeared later to add some reality.

'Morning Steve, sleep well?' he asked.

'Yes, OK,' Steve replied.

'So, a few more things; avoid Officer Rapton. He's just pure bastard, hates everyone, and Officer Peston.'

'Is he pure bastard too?'

'No, he's the only one that knows what he's doing! Nothing gets past him. He's totally on the ball, served fifteen years in the proper prison service, Cat A.'

'So is there much to get past him?'

'Oh yeah, you wouldn't believe it! There's not enough of them you see, as well as most of them being crap, so we run rings round them! Get this; last year a guy recced outside via his contacts and convinced the Doc that he needed a hospital appointment. Then when they took him out cuffed up, he persuaded them to stop at a motorway service station for a piss. He'd chosen the station in advance and one of his gang had got a job there as a cleaner. The guy had 'adapted' a toilet cubicle to have an escape panel at the back, so when the officer thought he was oh so clever and used the closet chain to allow the prisoner an extension to his handcuffs to use the toilet, he simply used an Allen key he'd had smuggled in earlier to open the hatch, access bolt croppers, cut the chain and disappear. When the officer got jumpy and asked him if he was OK and got no reply, he tugged on the chain and it flew out of the cubicle! He panicked, peered over the edge and couldn't believe his eyes! Later when the place was awash with uniforms, the cleaner signalled the all clear and the prisoner walked out of the cubicle calm as you like wearing yellow waterproof trousers, a high vis jacket and a yellow builder's hat that were previously stashed there, and together they walked straight out without attracting even a glance! He's not been caught since incidentally, word has it he's abroad now, and at least the officer did get sacked in that case; one less numpty for them to worry about!'

Steve couldn't believe it, he thought that could never happen where he'd just come from. You couldn't fart without somebody recording it on some tick sheet somewhere.

Steve was quite looking forward to meeting a whole range of new staff in a perverse sort of way. At least it broke the monotony. More induction inevitably followed with introduction to education, programmes, OMU, various work projects, healthcare, the multi-faith centre and the drugs and alcohol team. It did look all very shiny.

Later he was escorted to OMU for a first one to one appointment. The probation officer was Carl

Jones, a little man in his fifties with grey hair and a moustache. He was very open and straight to the point.

'Hi Steve, I'm Carl; I'm your new OS. I gather this was a rush move? I've spoken to Kirsty at Ashcourt, who sends her best wishes by the way, and got a picture of how things went there. So you tell me in your own words what happened, why you are here and what you make of your sentence so far?'

Steve paused and took a long breath. He explained about the situation in Cyprus, how in retrospect he had become 'obsessive' about this guy Markou and had taken it on himself, wrongly as it turned out, to sort him out. How he had observed him trafficking people onto the island and had gone to confront him in his bar/restaurant. How he had failed to think any of that through, how the situation had got out of hand, resulting in Markou's henchman getting killed. Steve still didn't even know the poor guy's name. How the authorities had closed in from both sides and how that had resulted in his life sentence. He told Carl that he still believed that he wasn't actually responsible for the death, and how his CO had supported him. He talked of the work he had done with Kirsty and Lucy and the progress he thought he'd made. He talked of his aspirations for the future and that he wanted to get out.

'OK Steve, that's helpful. I got a positive picture about you from Ashcourt. I've looked at your sentence plan and we'll need to amend that. You are into the third year of your sentence now, on a ten year tariff, so the concentration here in Farm Hill has got to be making sufficient progress to transfer to Cat C. You will need to do some work here on alcohol awareness, possibly the CALM course on managing anger and your emotions, continue your education and do some vocational training. The workshops when all up and running will be excellent. At the moment there's only gardens, an industrial wood and metal work shop and some light assembly work. Here is a pack for you to complete in your cell to give me some idea of how you think and how you are getting on. OK? So complete that for me before next time.'

Steve felt quite positive about the meeting. Much as he had enjoyed Kirsty and particularly Lucy's company last time, it was good to be able to speak to a bloke. The sentence plan sounded reasonable so Steve almost felt enthused.

Steve started to work with the Drug and Alcohol Team. He wasn't into drugs but accepted that when available he did tend to drink too much, albeit along with 95 percent of the rest of the battalion! He enquired about further education and signed up for a GCSE package covering Maths, English, History and Environmental Science. He figured if he was going to get on when released he needed to improve his education and get some qualifications. He was allocated a work place in gardens again and was told by programmes that he was on the list for CALM, but he was not likely to get a place yet and maybe not for several years, such was the demand.

Steve settled into his new environment. It certainly was different. He could see some of the old hands pulling all sorts of stunts but tried to keep out of it. However there was a distinctly unsavoury aspect to Farm Hill that Steve didn't like, hadn't seen before in prison and was being careful not to react to, at least not too soon. He was sure that he had heard a conversation between a prisoner and an officer and later seen direct evidence of bribes and corruption. Steve said nothing to anyone. He reckoned the prisoner wanted good reports to fast track out and the officer was prepared to falsify the records to 'give him a helping hand.' Large sums of money seemed to be involved. This time Steve thought carefully; it wasn't his business and if he reported it who could he trust and would he be believed? He concluded that to report it would probably only make life difficult for him and as this particular 'arrangement' didn't affect him directly he decided he was best just to leave it alone. He thought he could mention it to Pedro, but he probably knew anyway and what was the point?

At work in gardens Steve got on well with the instructor, Mr Bagshaw. Steve liked the distraction and the exercise as well as being outside. He soon was given some trust and responsibility to help oversee the chicken hutch building project. The plan was to house one hundred laying birds. Eggs could be used in the kitchens and sold to staff.

Compost all went back into the ground and with the garden and the poly tunnels a fair amount of food was grown. Some of it was also sold direct to the public via an outside shop in the grounds on a Cat C prison on the same site. Obviously Steve hadn't seen it but understood that it sold food grown by prisoners, and art work and crafts which raised money for victim support charities. Mr Bagshaw told him that one Cat C had a working kitchen staffed by prisoners with a restaurant that was open to the public called 'The Clink'!

In talking to other prisoners Steve found that although he thought that he'd had a hard life it was nothing compared to a lot of these guys. Many it seemed weren't very bright and probably were taking the rap for others, or were left standing when the police arrived. Others obviously had mental health problems; extreme anxiety, agitation, chronic depression and so on. Many had serious drink problems and would do anything for alcohol, including continually trying to scavenge fruit and sugar to make hooch. Many had experienced all kinds of shit, violence, abuse, you name it. He didn't meet many out and out bad guys, but there were some. Also lots of foreigners, from all over the world, often just young kids looking to make a living on drugs and got caught. Some of those guys had incredibly long sentences, he thought.

Matt, for example, was one of his work party. A quite withdrawn lad from Bolton, he didn't say much, but Steve guessed he was in for drugs. He looked worn by years of abuse. He also had scars all up his arm from cutting himself. Self harm they called it; Steve didn't really understand what that was about, why cut yourself? Matt had just been allocated to gardens. He'd been sacked from his last job for doing 'fuck all' and then refusing to go. He had seven days Cellular Confinement for it.

'Morning, Matt. OK?' enquired Steve the following day. 'Ready for a day's work then, mate?'

'You can fuck off! I didn't get any sleep last night; the sod in the next cell keeps his music on too loud and tries to sing! I'm knackered and I don't like this garden shit anyway.'

'What type of shit do you like then Matt?' asked Steve, trying to jolly him along.

'Nothing. Why do we have to work? We're banged up, aren't we? Ain't that enough?' he croaked back.

'Hey, come on, this at least takes your mind off things.'

'That's what drugs are for, mate. My mom was a tart and my dad was in and out of nick, then he left and my mom didn't want me, she kept my sister as she felt at least she could be a tart too later, but I went into care. I kept running away and they kept sending me to different places. I just got into thieving and glue and stuff, till I found drugs. I love 'em, but they fuck you up. What drugs do you do Steve?' Matt asked.

'No, I'm not into drugs, but I did like a drink.'

'What? Never done drugs? What, never? I've never known anyone who's never done drugs...no shit...you real?' Matt said in disbelief.

'I can get you some if you want Steve, what would you like to try first, mate?'

Steve struggled to convince him that he really wasn't interested in drugs, but they did laugh. Steve got to quite like Matt, he imagined that he had stayed in the army and got that Lance Corporal's stripe and that Matt had been posted to his section and he had to look after him. Not that Matt ever would have made a soldier! Steve tried to help and encourage him, laughed a lot and put up with his unreliability, his grumpy moods and black thoughts. Matt would routinely tell Steve that he was going to top himself that night then rumble along the next morning as if he'd said nothing!

One day Matt seemed particularly low. He said very little but Steve could tell. After a while Matt shared that he'd had a letter from his mother. He showed it to Steve with tears in his eyes. Steve read it. It was barely legible, but it said how proud she was that his 16 year old sister had started earning a living on the game and it included an indecent photograph of her. She went on that he needn't think that he could come back home after his sentence because they were too busy and they needed his room for some of the other girls to work in. Steve was shocked and could see the pain in Matt's eyes.

'What sort of a fucking mother sends her only son a letter like this!' Matt cried out with tears rolling down his cheeks, as he kicked out at the chicken shed, readily dismantling the pitifully small amount of progress that he had managed so far that day.

Mr Bagshaw came across to see what was wrong and unfortunately for him copped for a real mouthful of vile expletives. Matt had lost it and officers started arriving. Steve tried to calm him down, not wanting to see him be dragged off to the Seg, kicking and screaming. The first officer grabbed Matt roughly and Steve objected putting him straight on his back, then others arrived and a messy huddle formed and they all ended up on the floor rolling in the mud and completely smashed the embryonic chicken hut. Mr Bagshaw stood out of it and couldn't help but laugh, which probably didn't help the group of wound up young muscle bound officers to recover their composure.

That little escapade cost Steve and Matt seven days CC each. None of the officers could say for certain who had done what, so the adjudication concluded that both Steve and Matt had lost control and were equally culpable. It wasn't him that had lost control, Steve thought looking at the officers, but thought he'd best keep that to himself. As it turned out seven days afforded some time to get stuck into his GCSE work and he read as much as he could and wrote a few pieces of work, as well as topping up his press up count. Poor Matt did not cope as well with confinement and self harmed quite badly. When Steve saw him next he was still very subdued.

'How does that make you feel Steve, when your mother rejects you again and writes to tell you how well she's doing by forcing her daughter into prostitution!'

He was still very raw and very angry.

'What would your dad say Matt?' Steve asked.

'Probably "How much does she charge?"' he replied. 'My dad just looked after number one; he drank and fought and stole and just fucked things up,' said Matt with a sense of bitter resentment.

Sadly, Steve was to discover that Matt's experience of life was far more typical than his. Lots of the guys he met he regarded as fuck ups and losers. At least like the army there was always a tendency to descend into black humour just to get by. There was no limit to the crudity and depravity available. The way some of the guys talked about women made even Steve cringe, and how they talked about staff behind their back. Some guys could present as nice as pie, but would walk away from a conversation and turn in an instant to blame all their misfortune on the member of staff or 'the system.' Others were always looking for the next scam, like the fisherman looking for the perfect catch, but that too usually ended up like the one that got away.

Chapter 9

Anya and Rasha settled in London in a very compact modest flat. The law firm turned out to be a really good move. They helped Rasha with her basic education and encouraged her to take further qualifications in business administration. For Anya this was a big change. She was used to conducting her own affairs as a sole practitioner, but now she was part of a much bigger team. She was trying to adapt to her new setting and take on the wider brief of specialising in immigration, asylum and deportation cases.

Now that Steve had moved in Cat B, they were keen to visit. All obstacles had now been cleared and it was easier for Steve to apply for a legal visit for his 'legal team' than get permission for individual personal visits. Also, he was now deemed reliable enough for open visits, so they could meet and actually touch and look at each other in the eye without a glass screen. Rasha was still excited and still very sure and determined in her own mind that destiny had brought her and Steve together and that she was not going to let him go. Although not wanting to acknowledge it, she did also remind herself of Anya's words of caution. Rasha was now nineteen years old and a very different young woman than the bedraggled teenager that Steve had first encountered in the brothel. She had grown in confidence, her basic spoken English was good, she was much healthier, fuller figured and her general appearance was far more appealing and attractive.

Steve still felt some sense of misgivings, but had arranged the visit. He was conscious that he hadn't seen either of these women since the trial. Yes, they had kept in touch, but his memory of particularly Rasha was fairly vague by now. He did wonder how she was getting on, how she would look now and how he would feel when meeting her again.

The day of the visit had finally arrived and Steve had dressed in the best kit he could muster. He had been kept on the wing and off work in readiness for a morning visit. Being legal visits, most of the other guys he assumed would not have the same personal connection with their lawyers. Some would be seeking appeals or some other legal process to ease their passage through their sentence.

'OK Mr Mantel, I'll take you to the visits room now,' announced the officer sharply.

The normal search procedures were gone through and Steve was left in the waiting area with one other guy.

'You waiting for your brief, mate?' he enquired.

'Yeah, that's right.'

'Appeal, is it? They got me bang to rights, but then I found out that the silly bastards hadn't followed all the rules right, so my solicitor reckons she can get me off! Joke eh?' the other prisoner shared with him proudly.

The door opened.

'Mantel, you can come in now,' called the officer.

Steve rose and walked cautiously into the room and was allocated a table and told to wait. After a nervous five minutes, he could see two women entering the far end of the room, both smartly dressed. Anya looking distinctive, but slightly more westernised than when he saw her last. As they approached, he blinked. He couldn't believe what he saw as Rasha swaggered like a model walking towards him. As she got closer, memories of that night came flooding back, the power of that wave of emotion that had led him to gather her up and take her out of that dreadful place all came back. He was right to have done what he did, but there was also something else, something intangible that had drawn him to her; something he couldn't quite explain. As she approached and their eyes met, he knew. He knew without question, without fear of contradiction, he just knew. They all stopped in their tracks for a moment to take stock. Anya held out her hand warmly.

'Hello Steve, it's great to see you, you look really well!' she remarked, but he only had eyes for Rasha.

'Thank you, good to see you, too,' he replied politely shaking her hand.

Rasha interjected, 'Hi Steve, I've been so, so looking forward to this moment... Now I don't know what to say!'

'Wow!' Steve replied. 'Rasha, what a transformation... You...you look stunning!' Steve spoke softly.

'Thank you. You look good yourself,' she replied. Awkwardly they took each other's hands and just stood staring into each other's eyes and then embraced and she pecked his cheek. Steve desperately wanted to respond, but this just wasn't the moment and they stumbled to sit down.

They talked about Cyprus, about Anya and Rasha's new life, their journey to London and about Steve's experiences in prison. Rasha and Steve quietly held hands under the table. He felt like a daft kid, but he was conscious that it was a professional visits day and that much as he wanted to, it just wasn't appropriate to be all over her. He would have to wait. Rasha talked about her aspirations for the future and her hopes and dreams. Anya even managed to get some discussion with Steve about his case, but his mind was clearly on other things.

When their allotted time was up, Anya parted with a smile and a crisp handshake. Rasha and Steve stood again and gazed at each other; longing, hoping, waiting. They embraced, but had to part and she had to go. As she left, it was Rasha who simply said, 'I'll wait Steve... I'll wait…'

And then she was gone. He thought of all the things that he could have said, all the things that he wanted to say, but for now it was all too late. Steve was escorted back to the wing and the officer asked him how it had gone.

'Possibly the most important meeting in my life, Sir...' he replied calmly.

'Then good!' replied the officer, not knowing why.

****

It was time to meet the psychologist, Natalie Graham. She had read Steve's file and was looking forward to meeting him. She wanted to concentrate on his anger and depending on his progress make a fresh assessment about the need for the CALM course. Steve was brought to meet her in an interview room and by now was used to the likely format of the meeting.

'Hi Steve, I'm Natalie Graham, one of the psychologists here. I will be working with you, picking up from where Lucy left off and trying to make some progress with you on your emotional management. Is that OK?'

'Yes, that's fine, Miss,' Steve replied.

Lucy had conducted some tests and assessments to give her a framework to work in. She asked him what made him angry, how he recognised those feelings, how he dealt with them and if he could point to any examples in his prison experience of being challenged and either controlling his emotions effectively or losing control.

Steve described how he could get passionate about things, take on too much and sometimes act too impulsively. How he had tried simple techniques like counting to ten, to walk away and how 'Stop and Think' had helped him become more considered and reflective.

'OK. I see you have one recent adjudication for fighting. What was that about and could you have handled it differently?'

'Yeah, I could. Basically another prisoner was struggling and I felt sorry for him and tried to take him under my wing. I suppose I got too involved and then tried to protect him when it all went tits up,' he replied.

'Yes, OK. So what did you learn from that?'

'That the system fucks you over again, do you mean?'

'No, what was in your control that you could have done differently?'

'I could have left him to suffer on his own, is that what you want?'

'No, come on Steve, think! This is important. Could you have helped him in a different way that might not have resulted in you and maybe him getting into a brawl?'

'Yes I suppose so. So on this occasion I fucked it up, OK? But there have been others I have walked away from,' said Steve starting to get emotional.

'OK Steve. Look, you don't need to be so defensive, we all make mistakes. We just have to learn from them. Failure to learn from mistakes is a common characteristic amongst offenders; some just get stuck in groove and can't or won't shift, I expect better from you... Think about it, you could have called Mr Bagshaw over earlier instead of trying to handle it all yourself. You could have stepped aside when the officers arrived. We have choices Steve, so don't duck it, make the right decisions for you. Right, I want you to keep an anger diary from now on. Every time you feel angry I want you to record why, what you did about it and how it turned out. Then we can discuss it. You really need to crack this one if you want to move on, OK? So I don't want to see any more adjudications, warnings or negative entries. I want calm, responsible, pro-social behaviour, examples of trust and positive reports. Got it?' Natalie said firmly.

'OK, Miss, I think so.'

'I think so isn't good enough, Steve. Now have you got it?'

'Yes Miss!' Steve responded, almost saluted and marched out.

Fucking 'ell, he thought, where did they get her from? I'm not going to get anything past her!

Steve did dutifully keep the anger diary and it seemed to work. The mere act of recording his feelings made him more conscious of his choices and he did feel calmer. Several instances occurred when he could have just lost it but he *chose* not to. He was pleased with his progress and hoped it would satisfy his exacting tutor.

Over time Natalie got what she wanted. She was able to chart progress in Steve and he did successfully avoid any further trouble for six months. He also got positive comments from his education tutor for his commitment to his GCSEs and from Mr Bagshaw for his work in the gardens. He even seemed to have had a positive impact on helping Matt come to terms with his anger and resentment. At the end of the process she concluded that he was no longer a priority candidate for CALM and probably didn't need the course now. Steve was pleased. So was Rasha who demanded regular reports on his progress and helped to motivate him to keep on track.

Anya wrote with encouragement after their visit. She was very insightful. She had sensed that it had gone well, particular from Rasha's point of view. She hadn't stopped talking about Steve all the way home. Anya was really pleased privately that Steve had responded so well and had not rejected her. Anya encouraged Steve that he was doing well and moving forward. She also told him all about the little boy that he had rescued. Given that they were all to move to England, Anya had settled on an English name and had decided to call him Ben. She sent a photo. Steve obviously couldn't remember how he looked in any detail but was pleased to see him now. He looked well. Anya believed that he was now about ten and ready to engage with school. His general development had no doubt been impaired by his experiences, but Anya considered that he was bright and would do well with encouragement.

Steve was really proud of Anya for offering Ben a home and he looked forward to meeting him again some day. Another indication of injustice struck him; OK, the henchman had died but Steve had saved Ben, yet he still faced a life sentence for taking a life that he maintained that he didn't, but got no credit for saving one.

Rasha had also written a very warm, loving letter, allowing herself to express some of her feelings. Steve was taken aback by the intensity of the tone of the letter, but pleased nevertheless. He sat down and attempted to reply. He wasn't very good at expressing his feelings, he felt, but made several attempts before he sent anything.

Letters continued between them and Rasha started a regular pattern of visits, as a personal visitor and not as a professional. That allowed them greater opportunity for expressing their feelings although obviously there was a limit in an open public visits room. They grew ever closer, sharing experiences and daring to look forward to the future.

Rasha was gaining confidence at work and doing well. She had achieved several promotions and was contemplating buying a small place of her own. The law firm encouraged staff to do so, as an incentive for recruitment and retention by offering preferential terms for finance. Given the property prices in London, this was the only way most staff could aspire to pursue ownership. Rasha was also thinking ahead in wanting a have a place ready to offer Steve a base when the time came to consider resettlement. She knew about the process having researched it extensively at work, that Steve would be considered for periods of temporary release in order to demonstrate trust and adjust back to life in the community before being finally released by the Parole Board on life licence with probation supervision. Steve was impressed by her knowledge. In fact she was way ahead of him and provided a source of information to enable him to prompt the system from time to time.

The CO also wrote and visited periodically. His business was doing well and he was still trying to influence the army to take a sympathetic and supportive view when the time came for consideration for release. He also relayed some stories of his adventures, including a high level ski expedition in Norway, pot holing in Cambodia and a river journey in North Africa. Lance had found no shortage of people prepared to pay a premium for an extreme guided adventure experience. He was starting to form a solid nucleus of experts that he could call on to help; all independent people who would come along on pay as you go terms, without any commitment to permanent staff. Some were ex-military, mostly Special Forces but others were just young adventurers in their own field; climbers, canoeists and the like. Lance knew from his military experience that you also need good logistics and medical support. One of the ex-SAS guys was a good solid all round medic, so they had tended to rely on him at the sharp end and negotiate insurance for hospital back up if required at the scene. This had proved to be challenging in the more remote parts of the world, so there was a genuine sense of adventure with these trips, albeit at a risk. Lance had developed a network of contacts for logistics and a small staff that were UK based to organise transport, equipment, insurance etc, and be a point of contact with families if needs be. There were also the business end to update the website, take calls and bookings.

****

Out of the blue Anya wrote with some unexpected news from Cyprus. She informed Steve that Stephan Markou had been killed on the Island. Apparently he had been perceived to have become greedy and others further up the criminal supply chain had taken offence. Involvement by Russian or Chinese criminal gangs was suspected in orchestrating the movement of people using Markou's sphere of influence. His body had been found in every room of his very large house. Someone had wanted to make a very firm point. The reaction in Cyprus, Anya reported, had been mixed - from outcry at the terrible loss of a local civic dignitary, to undercurrents of a less sympathetic nature given the long standing rumours and concerns about his activities.

Steve could hardly express regret or sympathy. He hoped that his death had been painful and protracted. It led to some odd feelings. In a perverse sort of way he felt vindicated, not of course that the system would see it that way and open the gates, but he hoped that the politics behind his case would be eased by this news.

Chapter 10

Things went well for Steve in Cat B. He understood that it was another staging point and he had complied with his sentence plan, learnt something along the way and felt ready to move on. He successfully completed his GCSE course, passing all four subjects. Steve wasted no time in signing up to do two A levels in History and Politics. His experience in gardens had been useful, although he had no intention of becoming a gardener, but he had taken the chance to develop his leadership skills and demonstrate a capacity for responsibility and trust. He had related well to Carl and had tolerated Natalie. He had also met his outside probation officer from his home area, although he understood that he would not be supervising him on release if he resettled in London.

Steve warmed to Rasha's idea of settling in the Capital. He was grateful to her for her commitment and support. Contact with his family had diminished over time. Steve hadn't heard from his father or brother for over twelve months now and letters from his mother had become less frequent. The truth was they had pretty much run out of things to say and more pressing problems were taking priority. In essence, Steve had become out of sight and out of mind. In a way this had helped him decide that there was no future for him back home and that he was best to start again somewhere new. The CO was also based in the South of England, so he was content to accept Rasha's offer. Rasha had by now moved into her own very modest two bedroom flat in one of the relatively cheaper areas. She was so pleased that Steve had agreed, and set about furnishing and equipping a home with them both in mind. She sent him regular photographs and shared ideas of décor and furnishings when she visited. It soon felt like Steve almost lived there already. Rasha was very self-disciplined in the way she managed her money. She had not been able to find any trace of her family back in Egypt or she would have happily tried to support them. Instead she lived a quiet life; ate modestly, rarely went out socially except with Anya and diligently saved as best as she could.

After nearly two years in Farm Hill, it was decided that it was time to move on. Probation and psychology had helped him develop his understanding of the offence and his own behaviour and Steve had taken opportunities to learn and to practice new skills and approaches. He had accepted a more balanced and realistic view of his own culpability and the impact on others and was less inclined to see himself as a victim. After some discussion, the authorities agreed that Steve was ready for a move to Cat C and a transfer was approved. Although it would have helped to move further south towards London he was allocated a place at Castle Gate, a traditional public sector Cat C prison on the same site.

After several false starts, delays and disappointments, eventually a move date was confirmed, and on the day Officer Rapton unlocked and barked his orders to Mantel to pack his kit.

'Come on Mantel, it's time for you to fuck off! Off you go - someone else is waiting for your cell!'

Steve was escorted to reception in a rush in order, like the army, to 'hurry up and wait.' One of the governors was walking through, and whilst kit was being checked Steve took the opportunity to briefly mention to him that one of his officers was on the take. He seemed to take it in. Security procedures were gone through, before unusually he was led through the gate, briefly to meet the outside world, cross a car park carrying his worldly goods in two large transparent plastic sacks and through another gate to another new start. Again all the kit that had just been checked was checked again and the same security procedures gone through. Steve did feel some greater sense of familiarity with the traditional uniforms as against some flashy corporate logo, and felt that he was back in a 'proper prison'.

As the name implied, Castle Gate was an old style building, pretty much to a classic castle design with an inner courtyard, but with a whole labyrinth of added 'temporary' portacabin buildings dotted about in no particular order.

The induction officer asked the usual questions but also tried to help set the scene about what it meant for a lifer to have got to Cat C.

'OK. Steve Mantel isn't it? We've been expecting you for a while. I gather your sentence has gone pretty well so far. You'll find the difference in Cat C is that we expect you to do more for yourself. Most of your identified work should have been done by now and we will sit back and watch to see how you conduct yourself, how you cope and see if you are ready, in time, to move to open conditions. Remember, it's a new situation now and staff will be constantly assessing you. Any questions?'

'Open conditions is Cat D, yeah?' Steve asked.

'Yes, that's right, but let's concentrate on Cat C first. If you wait in that holding bay, one of the officers will point out where your accommodation is and you can go and settle in.'

'You mean I can just walk there myself?' Steve remarked.

'Yes, welcome to Cat C! As I said, you will be expected to be more independent. Prisoner movement here is pretty well free. It's a small prison. We have no sex offenders here or any vulnerable prisoner facilities, so by and large you can move around within the walls. You take your self to work and to any appointments. When you meet a locked gate, you just wait for a member of staff who will check your appointment card and let you through if everything is in order. Understand?'

Steve was beginning to. It was a strange feeling, like a kid in a new school looking for a friend from one of the big boys! He had overcome some tests and challenges in his time, but he felt strangely anxious at the sudden prospect of such relative freedom and indeed responsibility. Was it a sign that he was getting his life back, he wondered?

After a modest wait he was let through the door, bags in hand clearly identifying him as a new boy and sent off towards B Wing. It didn't prove to be too difficult to find; once in the central part of the prison, wings were identified around the square, with B Wing in front of him. Steve found the entrance and as instructed waited. An officer came by.

'Afternoon, just arrived?'

'Yes, that's right.'

'OK then, come on let's find out which cell you are in.'

They went through together into an old landing style block that did smell a little institutional after the bright modern unit in Farm Hill. Steve was allocated a cell on the third floor and after some basic induction covering pretty much what the officer in reception had told him, he was back in the security of a cell. This one was pretty grubby, it needed a good clean, so before he unpacked Steve asked for a bowl of water and set about washing it down. Snot, spit, dust and general grime was everywhere but he did manage to wash away the worst of it. Steve laughed to himself as he thought, I'll just nip out to B&Q this evening and get some fresh paint and wallpaper!

The following day induction continued. Steve knew broadly what to expect by now. He was allocated to a light assembly workshop initially, which he understood was tedious and unpopular, so everyone had to start there to make up the numbers. The education department seemed limited but Steve hoped to be able to pick up his A Level work where he left off. In theory that was how modules were meant to work. He had an appointment with his offender supervisor, this time a prison and not a probation officer, and talking to another lifer gathered that there had been a series of complaints against this officer for what sounded like straight incompetence. The other lifer had put it more succinctly, that 'he was just a fucking wanker and was out of his depth'!

When Steve met Officer O'Brien it didn't take long to see what the guy meant. He seemed hesitant and gave the impression that he would be more comfortable walking the landings jangling keys than grappling with risk assessment and sentence planning. Nevertheless Steve felt that he must try to work with him and keep an open mind. They reviewed his sentence plan and agreed that a risk assessment of 'Medium' was appropriate at this stage. Mr O'Brien seemed concerned that Steve hadn't done the CALM course and seemed to think that the Parole Board would want him to have done it. Steve tried to explain that he had completed appropriate one to one work with the vociferous psychologist at Farm Hill, but he didn't seem to want to listen. He agreed with further education and vocational training and tried to encourage Steve to go for a trade.

'If you have a trade lad, you'll never be out of work,' he said.

Try saying that to miners and shipbuilders, Steve thought. Officer O'Brien may not be his cup of tea, but Steve felt that he could work with that. There were no probation officers in this prison.

Steve took the opportunity to write to his outside probation officer back home and keep a link. After a while a letter came back saying that he had been reallocated to a new officer already. He was now with Rachael Mohamed. Steve tried to ring her several times, but she always seemed to be on leave, off sick, on a course or in court so he gave up in the end.

****

Rasha was due to visit again, and Steve was keen to tell her all about the new prison. He was getting to realise how much he missed her and the strength of feeling that was developing between them. As he sat in the visits room waiting he dared to dream about a future together.

When Rasha arrived she looked stunning and Steve could see that she was attracting attention from the male staff booking people in. He wanted to intervene and tell them to back off, but managed to think better of it.

Rasha seemed only mildly irritated as she approached with a broad smile. They embraced and kissed. It felt so good to feel her warmth in his arms again and just to be near her.

They talked at great speed, exchanging news about Steve's new location and Rasha's new flat. He felt so proud of her. It was beginning to feel like she was the centre of his world. Rasha explained to him about his next hurdle.

'Steve, you are entitled to town visits here where an officer takes you out for a day to a local town just to start familiarising yourself with the outside world, to use public transport, handle money, that sort of thing.'

'OK.'

'Then you have an Oral Hearing with the Parole Board. This is a big step honey, you mustn't mess it up. Only they can decide to order open conditions then you can move again to an open prison and start to work outside and adjust back to normal life with regular weekends at home. Just think of that, we can spend weekends together; it will be heaven!'

'Yes! Don't worry, I'll get it right!' Steve assured her.

'Oh, and you must remember to request an open prison in the south. I have looked on the internet and there is a men's open prison about thirty miles from me called Bardon Wood. That's the one you want.'

'OK,' Steve agreed and they held hands over the table and dared to dream; they imagined a whole weekend together, walked through her flat in their minds, planned menus, walked by the river and tried to catch up on lost time in their love-making. They were lost in the dream when sadly time was called and they had to part again. It hurt, but the visit would keep them both going until the next time.

Steve returned to his cell elated. How lucky he was, how in love he was falling, how good it felt.

The following day he had an appointment with his offender manager from home, Rachael Mohamed, who he had not met before. She would be writing his reports for the Parole Board, so he felt it was vital to make a good impression. Steve knew Rasha would expect nothing less.

On arrival in the visits room the same two officers were on duty who had been there yesterday when Rasha arrived. He heard them talk.

'Hey, remember that bitch yesterday with the legs up to her armpits?' said one.

'Yeah, did you see the tits on it?' said the other. 'We could arrange a strip search for her, looked like she needed it to me!'

'Yeah, I'd give her one!'

Suddenly he fell to the floor when a massive blow to his face connected. Steve had heard enough and had reacted. No one was going to talk about his Rasha like that, the animals, the bastards. He was incensed! He felt so angry. How could staff behave like this, he thought!

Before Steve had time to deliver the same greeting to the second officer he was surrounded by uniforms, bent over, and was on his way to the Seg.

He knew he'd blown it, all the hopes and dreams gone in an instant. He felt gutted, so disappointed with himself.

In the Seg he could talk through all the things he should have done. He could have challenged the officers assertively, he could have written down what they said and made a formal complaint, he could have walked away. He *should* have remembered to *stop* and *think*. Doubt came into his mind. Was he really ready to move on? Did he really deserve Rasha? Would she forgive him...?

The Seg is a place to cool off, so Steve was just left to stew. He couldn't harm himself or anyone else in the allotted cell. He was just left with his thoughts; all that time, all that effort just blown away in a furious moment. How stupid he was, how disappointed he felt. He was gearing himself up to make a good impression with his offender manager from home whom he had never met, and now she would be driving back up north without even seeing him. What an impression that would make! Assaulting an officer, no doubt about it, he had blown it big time, and he'd be back in Cat B by the morning he convinced himself.

An officer entered the cell and asked him if he wanted a phone call. He was grateful and thought that he'd better phone Anya rather than Rasha.

Anya was disappointed to hear his story but listened as Steve explained what was said, what happened and how he felt. Anya didn't respond.

'I've blown it, haven't I ?' he said.

'Well, it is going to be difficult to argue our way out of this one, but all I can do is try,' she conceded. 'Have you told Rasha?'

'No, not yet; I thought it would be better to wait for the outcome.'

'OK, up to you. She'll be terribly upset, you know that don't you?'

'Yes, I know. It makes me wonder if I really deserve her Anya?'

'Well, that's a matter for her Steve; you'll have to sweat it out and wait,' Anya replied, trying to make an impact while knowing there was no way Rasha would ever reject him.

'Can you intervene on my behalf, Anya? I really need you now,' Steve almost begged.

'I don't know yet Steve. You'll have to leave it with me for now. I'll let you know.' And the call ended.

Steve sat up on an empty bench in a stark cell, confined, trapped like an animal with a plastic plate and a dry portion of nondescript pie, chips and bullet peas on his lap, which he really didn't feel like eating. He felt like he wanted to go out and get absolutely smashed with his mates and wake to a hell of a hangover. Instead he faced a long night alone to await his fate.

In the morning the governor herself came to see him.

'Good morning, I'm Governor Woodward, the number one governor here. I've come to see you about yesterday's events. I'm sorry, it should never have happened,' she said calmly.

'Good morning Ma'am,' Steve piped up, not believing his ears. Had she really just said that, he thought?

'My officers should never have behaved like that towards your partner, for which I feel deeply ashamed and can only sincerely apologise. I shall of course be writing to her myself to apologise to her directly. Not of course that I can condone your response, but maybe I can understand it. Anyway, more of that later. I need to share some very sensitive information with you.' She went on to explain that she had been concerned about a culture of sexism in the prison that had been allowed to develop over the years without being challenged. She continued that she was aware of a catalogue of complaints against these two officers in particular concerning inappropriate behaviour towards female visitors, ordering unjustified strip searches and even an unsubstantiated allegation of rape of a female member of staff.

'As a result of all this I have been trying to gather sufficient evidence against these two men to dismiss them, but they have been clever, until now. Unbeknown to them they have been subject to camera surveillance for some time and both yesterday's comments and today's incident are both fully recorded on tape, including of course your part in it. As a result of which I am satisfied that I can now proceed with dismissal without fear of appeal or claim for compensation. They'll be gone and good riddens; there is no place in Her Majesty's Prison Service for officers who behave like that.'

Steve was dumbfounded. 'Ma'am, I'm so sorry for what I did, I shouldn't have reacted like that, and I too have no respect for your officers if they act like that, but should they really lose their jobs over me?'

'Oh don't kid yourself, it's not over you at all, this was just the final straw and there will be many members of staff here with cause to celebrate, including the senior officer whose daughter was I'm in no doubt raped by these men. Privately, many will think they are glad that someone struck out at them and only wished that you'd had longer!'

Steve couldn't believe what he was hearing.

'So Ma'am...'

'Yes, of course, so what will happen to you? Obviously I have to deal with you for assaulting an officer; he's got a broken nose and two good black eyes by the way. Regardless of the circumstances, it's the principal here that prisoners cannot assault staff without sanction, and staff must feel supported if they get injured in the course of their job. I have to consider therefore whether to send you immediately back to Cat B, which I must admit would be my normal course of action. In your case however, I'm prepared to keep you here, *but* you will have to serve a period in segregation with no visits and it will put your progress towards Cat D back by at least a year. More importantly if we are meant to be helping you to turn around, you really must learn from this to kerb that temper. I have to warn you that any further instances of violence could result in effectively throwing away the key, do you understand?'

'Yes Ma'am. Thank you Ma'am,' muttered Steve meekly, knowing that she was absolutely right and had been more than fair with him.

'OK, then we'll do that. You'll see me in adjudication later this morning. Expect 28 days.'

As Mrs Woodward walked away she pondered whether she had got the balance right. Dismissing the two unprofessional officers was the greater prize and she didn't want in any way to undermine her case against them, but she knew that her sanction against Mantel would be seen as light. She just hoped he repaid her by learning the lesson this time, before the Parole Board made their judgment. If not she risked looking exposed in their eyes. Either way the Parole Board would now take some convincing to sanction open conditions in the first hearing however well he did.

Once word got out about the whole incident, there was a mixed reaction. The area manager made it very plain to his governor that this had been her decision and if it turned out badly, effectively she'd be on her own. Most staff could see the sense of what she did and were very happy to see the back of their two colleagues, although for some it was just another opportunity to argue that the service had lost its way and just gone soft on crime. For one father in particular, whose daughter had left the service after feeling so let down after the rape incident, this was some sense of natural justice. He just wished that he had been the SO in charge of visits that day so that he could have delayed the response and left Mantel to do more damage. The governor's deputy had said to her, 'Blimey Margaret, that was a brave decision.' Which effectively meant that she thought it was reckless. For the prisoners, of course, this was one back against the system.

Sensing the reaction, Margaret Woodward chose to address it directly with her staff at the next All Staff Briefing soon after the incident. She went through the usual performance data, reassured staff that there were no current plans to close, re-role or privatise Castle Gate, and offered congratulations and thanks where they were due.

'Finally,' she said, 'I just wanted to refer to the recent incident of the dismissal of two officers and the response to prisoner Mantel. Firstly, I make no apology whatsoever for dismissing the two men. I want to make it perfectly clear that disrespectful behaviour, physical or sexual intimidation towards anyone by members of staff is completely unacceptable. I know that many of you have been deeply uncomfortable about their behaviour for some time. We must seek to create a culture of mutual respect, honesty and trust, where staff feel supported by my management and feel able to report bad practice.

'As regards Mantel, I can assure you that I thought long and hard about this before making my decision. He will serve an appropriate length of time in segregation and I ask you to be particularly vigilant about his behaviour with us thereafter, but we must also be fair, and there is no room for personal reactions to this case. Either way, the Parole Board will have the final say to judge the significance of this incident in the context of his overall performance, but be in no doubt, assaulting an officer will slow down his progress.'

She just hoped the message had got through.

****

Sitting in segregation, Steve was debating how he was going to explain all this to Rasha. He concluded that he could only be honest and started to write a letter. He explained what had happened, what he did and why, and the consequences of all that. For the first time, he wrote that he loved her and tried to apologise and promised to do all he could to retrieve the situation and not delay their plans to be together. He just hoped that she would understand. He also wrote to Anya in more official terms and explained all that had happened to her too.

When the letters arrived Rasha was at Anya's and hadn't started using her new address for correspondence yet. Anya knew their likely content and the impact they would have. She read her letter quickly and waited while Rasha took her letter upstairs as usual to read it in private. It wasn't long before she could hear the sound of sobbing and waited hoping Rasha would seek her attention for comfort. Reading between the lines it appeared to Anya that Steve had been lucky but she suspected that there would be a counter reaction and problems ahead. She could also see that to under play his part served the wider purpose of dismissing the rogue officers.

Ben was happily playing when Rasha came down stairs. She was calm, but visibly upset.

'Oh Anya, this is so hard. He did it for me, I know he did! I just wish that he had done it a different way! Will it destroy our chances of being together Anya? Please tell me that it won't!' she said with tears running down her face.

'I know, I know. That streak in him to just react is going to be difficult to kerb, but he needs to kerb it if he is to avoid further trouble. Do you think he realises that Rasha?' Anya responded sensitively, whilst Ben looked on bemused.

'Yes, I do, of course I do, but I just hope that he can do it Anya.'

She sat holding the letter, shaking and in tears. 'Oh and Anya, he says he loves me!'

Chapter 11

Senior Officer Fraser McGregor and Steve had started to talk on the wing regularly. Steve had told him his story and SO McGregor had disclosed some of his feelings about his daughter and how she was treated after the rape allegation. They had a connection. Steve had eventually been out on his first familiarisation visit to the local town, which had gone well. He didn't feel too alienated from real life. He was also progressing well with his studies and coping with the step up to A level.

It was the day of the second visit and there was tension in the air in the prison. In a small establishment you could feel it. The weather had been warm and the kitchens were old and kept having problems with power failure which lead to problems with the food being late or being spoiled. Spoiled more than usual that is. The combination of heat, tension and poor food can easily become critical in upsetting the delicate balance that holds a prison together.

On B Wing things were pretty much as normal, with arguments at the phone queue and the pool table. However one particular prisoner was boiling and SO McGregor hadn't picked it up. Charlie Sharp was generally regarded as fairly mad and not really prison material. He was serving life for murder of his partner, allegedly because she had served him a cup of cold tea one day when he was having one of his turns, and he'd stabbed her to death. He was volatile and unpredictable and today he was armed. He'd managed to find an ordinary metal piece of cutlery whilst cleaning the staff room and sharpened it to a point and mounted it on a makeshift handle. He knew that workmen were repairing a door frame and refurbishing a corridor space to make an extra office and that the corridor lead to a skylight with access to an area of flat roof. He reckoned the workmen could be distracted and that he could then get onto the roof. Charlie had always maintained that he hadn't killed his partner, but that some mystery intruder had entered their flat and done it. A sort of burglary gone wrong, but his story never stacked up and no one had ever believed him.

The wing was quiet. One officer had gone out on hospital escort, one was sick and the SO was in his office on the phone, that left just one officer on patrol, albeit with only two or three prisoners around, the others being at work. She was talking to one of the guys by the phone who was complaining that he could never get hold of his probation officer outside to talk to her.

Charlie saw his chance. He was the wing cleaner. He calmly put the knife in his pocket and walked up to the top landing with his broom, approached the remaining workman whilst the other two were having a tea break and swept past him, cleaning the corridor as he went. By the time he had reached a point under a sky light where prisoners would normally never be allowed access, SO McGregor who had seen him go upstairs smelt trouble. He left his office and run up to the top landing. Looking across the landing, he reckoned he knew what was in Charlie's mind and followed after him into the corridor where the workmen had been.

By then Charlie had managed to open the skylight and climb out onto the roof. The SO followed him, but Charlie had been cunning and had waited out of sight by the hatch and closed it behind him as he climbed through, trapping the SO on the roof with him.

SO McGregor could see that he had now walked straight into a hostage situation and it was too late to turn back He decided to play it cool, knowing how unpredictable Charlie was, and not just go for his radio to call for help. Charlie started ranting about how he'd been held in custody for years for something he didn't do and how he was going to show them all. He demanded his captive's radio and threw it to the crowd. Fraser McGregor had been in the service a long time and knew very well that an experienced, calm, cool head would out think the average prisoner any day. There were just the two of them and he reckoned Charlie was no match for him. So he waited and let him rant. He anticipated that emergency procedures downstairs were now well underway and he was right.

The workman had pressed the alarm bell. Officers were running, radios were screeching messages and the governor was collecting her team in the command suite. The local police and fire service were alerted and prison area office to stand by an emergency response team, i.e. prison officers specially trained and prepared dressed in riot gear.

The duty officer had run to the courtyard on hearing the alarm and the incident description. From there he could see Charlie on the roof playing to the small crowd that had now gathered. Other officers were marshalling prisoners back to their wings for lock up and a roll check. This was a vulnerable moment; if the prisoners refused, the duty officer knew they were in trouble.

On B Wing the workmen had secured the corridor onto the roof. Steve was left with Officer Jarrett, the young woman who had been talking to the prisoner by the phone, who she had managed to lock up in his cell, Steve guessed what had happened and quickly made a proposal.

'No time to explain Miss, but there is another way onto the roof, I can climb it I'm sure and could help get Officer McGregor down safely.'

'No, no, wait a minute. If they are up there, we'll have a whole team to negotiate and get them down safely, it's not a job for you.'

Meanwhile the governor's team was getting into action. They had been given a brief on Charlie's profile. She had called the doctor to give a view on his current mental state and the initial risk assessment was that Charlie could attempt to throw the SO off the roof or jump himself, with or without the SO, any of which would be likely to result in death or serious injury.

Reports were coming in that the police could arrive in numbers if required within 30 minutes, the fire service were on standby and were studying plans of the building in case they had to enter and area office could deploy an emergency response team in approximately 6 hours.

'Not good enough, far too slow,' the governor shouted to the radio operator. Tell them I need them at the gate in less than two hours.'

Prisoners were beginning to respond to the attempt to conduct an orderly move back to the wings, but some were hanging back in view of the roof and Charlie was playing to the audience.

'Hey you lot down there, lets have a fucking riot! What are you waiting for you wankers?' shouted Charlie to his fans. The message was potentially toxic.

Officer Jarrett on B Wing could follow proceedings on her radio and was in two minds. Steve was firmly in action mode and wanted to get on with it, but was also trying desperately to *think*. Steve could hear her radio too.

'Miss, sounds like Charlie is distracted by playing the fool. Doesn't that give us an opportunity to grab the initiative and use my plan to get Mr McGregor down?'

She was young and inexperienced and he was persuasive. She was beginning to be won over.

'Can I trust you? You might be part of the escape plan!'

'No, honesty, Miss, I've got too much to lose to pull a daft stunt like that.'

Then they smelt it, it was getting stronger, no doubt about it...*fire*!

'Come on Miss, that's the smell of smoke, someone has started a fire. This is serious now; we have to get him off that roof! There's no time to collect a whole team,' Steve shouted firmly.

'OK, let's try your plan,' she replied.

Steve quickly led her to a place where there was a small gap in the barbed wire on a corner, leading to the same flat roof.

'There it is, Miss,' he pointed out.

'You'll never climb over that!' she exclaimed.

'Oh yes I will!' he replied and set off, seemingly sticking to the wall like glue and managing to clamber steadily up towards the tricky part to span a seemingly impossible overhang. With some effort and expertise he was up and onto the roof. He lay flat and silent. Steve could see Charlie in front of him, approximately a hundred metres away. He was standing behind the SO, threatening him in some way and shouting challenges and abuse to the staff down below. The duty officer had a megaphone and was trying to engage with him, but Charlie had lost it and wasn't listening. Steve judged that this was critical; no way could he risk rushing Charlie from this position. His only option was to wait. Charlie soon tired of posturing to the officials below and let the SO go for a moment and returned towards the far edge of the roof to address his other audience.

He held out his arms as if addressing the crowd at the Glastonbury festival.

'Hey! I'm the King! I'm the fucking King!' he shouted down to them. They cheered and shouted back. Charlie loved it. He was now important, he was getting the attention.

Steve threw a small stone in the direction of Mr McGregor to attract his attention. By now Officer Jarrett had become concerned about the fire and had moved down to the courtyard before she feared that her route could be blocked off. She ran round to where the duty officer was standing, by which time he had noticed some movement on the roof. The SO was slowly moving away from Charlie, but there was another figure on the roof.

'Who the fuck's that!' the duty officer exclaimed, pointing to Steve who was crouching by now and beckoning the SO over towards him.

'It's Steve Mantel, Sir,' said Officer Jarrett, 'he showed me a route up onto the roof ,but you would need to be an accomplished climber to attempt it; he's going to try to bring Fraser down!'

'*What!* Are you telling me that you've let a prisoner go on the roof during an incident to launch some ill-conceived botched rescue plan?'

'Yes Sir, but it might just work while Charlie is playing to his audience, can't we just add to it by winding him up to keep him occupied, then I really think Mantel can do it.'

'I fucking hope you're right! Bloody hell- he could easily make it worse...! OK, he's committed, to carry on is probably the least bad option, at least for now. Come on let's try your distraction idea. With the addition of the fire there's no time to organise anything better right now. This better work or we'll both be hung out to dry!'

They ran round to face Charlie and the duty officer shouted up at him, 'Charlie you fool, come on down. You'll get life for this!'

'Fuck off!' he said, 'I'm not coming down.'

'Charlie, don't be stupid. I can help you. Come on lad; be sensible, this isn't going to get you anywhere.'

'I don't need your fucking help you tosser! Fuck off! I'm in charge now!' he replied, like a true performer. The officer tried to stay calm and keep him engaged. Charlie would listen for a while, then hurl insults, then return to play to his audience.

'Boys! I'm your man; I'm the Daddy!' Charlie shouted down.

Steve had by now established eye contact with SO McGregor, who was steadily moving towards him. Although this was all wrong, he did feel that he could trust Steve and that he offered a genuine chance to escape from Charlie. Steve quickly signalled him to follow and started to help him climb down the same route that he had used getting up. He hadn't fully appreciated how hard it was going to be to get down, especially for the SO who was no climber, also he hadn't factored in the fire, which was spreading faster than he had figured on a warm summer's evening.

Outside the gate by now a small army had gathered; police in riot gear ready to go in and a large number of fire fighters. The emergency response team was still on the road. Prison staff by now had some success in marshalling prisoners to safety. However, the fire was dictating that it was simply not safe to lock them all up in case it spread. Establishing a reliable roll call was proving to be difficult too. Prisoners were now being held in the gym. Not all prisoners had been moved away from the end of the building in order to maintain Charlie's attention, but by now he had noticed that his captive had moved and began to run across the roof to find him.

Steve and the SO were making good progress climbing down, but now reached the difficult part where the gap in the wire was and the over hang on the roof. Steve was guiding him down when Charlie appeared at the top and started hurling abuse, quickly followed by roof tiles from the adjoining pitched roof. As they rained down upon them they managed to duck for the most part but every so often one connected. A tile caught the SO on the shoulder and he slipped. Steve managed to grab his hand but was holding on himself with one arm and holding up the SO with his other hand. He summoned up all his determination and strength but he knew that he could not hold this for very long.

The governor ordered the riot police to move at that moment now that there was no further advantage in keeping prisoners by the building to keep Charlie's attention. Resistance proved to be nominal, and soon the stragglers had moved on towards the gym. Fire fighters could then deploy to deal with their aspect of the incident. Whilst fanning out over the area, some of the police officers and fire fighters noticed the precarious position Steve was in trying to hang onto the SO whilst getting pelted with masonry. Quickly, they formed around the area where he was likely to land and were able to call to Steve to let go and managed to catch the officer, breaking his fall. Steve followed and they were both alright. In the circumstances they simply followed instructions and moved quickly to the gym to join the others. The fighter fighters called for a ladder, and two police officers shimmied up the same route and grabbed Charlie before he could move away. No one wanted a protracted roof protest, so all were highly relieved to have secured Charlie at ground level. He was arrested and taken away. By then the governor was faced with the agonising decision whether to unlock all those prisoners that they had secured because of fear of fire and risk increasing the chances of losing control and seeing the situation deteriorate into chaos.

It wasn't long before the lead fire officer provided the answer.

Fortunately the fire proved to be more smoke than anything more serious. Someone had taken the opportunity to light some wet pallets and general rubbish stored at the back of the works department and no buildings were actually damaged, nor more importantly was anyone injured.

Fire fighters patrolled the prison until the lead officer was satisfied that he could report to the governor that it was safe to return all prisoners to their cells. Things were getting tense in the gym, everyone was crammed in and there was no scope for anything but to sit and wait, and prisoners aren't generally the most patient of people. A further logistical problem awaited the governor; the afternoons activities had disrupted normal routine and the kitchens hadn't been at work. She now faced trying to move most of her prisoners from the gym, encourage them to go quietly back to their cells, knowing that she then had no capacity to feed them. This was not a good recipe for calm and order.

'What are we going to do about feeding them all, George?' Margaret Woodward asked one of her senior managers. 'Send out for the biggest fish and chip order in history?'

'Don't worry Margaret, I thought of that while you were dealing with the main incident. The MOD had been put on standby to provide helicopter transport to bring in the emergency response team if necessary. As you said, potentially six hours by road would be far too slow. While I was speaking to them, I mentioned feeding and they offered to help. An army mobile kitchen has turned up outside and is currently preparing 600 hot meals, including all the variations for religion, preference and so on that the army are also used to now. It will probably be better than they normally get!'

'Bless you George, what would I do without you?'

Officers demonstrated their skills in dealing with upset prisoners with calm, professionalism and humour. Prisoners returned to their cells, by and large without a hitch.

'That was the best summer bonfire and street entertainment show I've seen in years, Boss, can we book it again for next year?' cried one prisoner to the staff.

'Of course Nobby! We'll try to get Robby Williams and the Queen guitarist, Brain May for the roof scene next year!' replied the officer.

'OK Boss!'

'We could combine it with the annual BBQ and beer festival as well, Sir!' said another.

'OK. Or how about a hog roast?'

The governor was anxious however to hear a confirmed roll check, to make sure no one had managed to disappear in the chaos. When eventually the numbers came through they were four short. One of course was Charlie Sharp who was now in police custody, but what about the other three?

'Have we accounted for hospital escorts and any ROTL or temporary transfers? And have we recovered that radio thrown from the roof, and has SO McGregor still got his keys?' she asked.

'Yes, Ma'am to the radio and the keys, the roll check is accurate Ma'am; we checked the figures several times before reporting to you. We are three missing.'

Whilst further checks and enquires were being made the governor went to check for herself that Fraser was OK, and to call in to thank Steve Mantel. She entered the gym as staff were just about finishing clearing up, she thought people looked tired but relieved, which she thought was about right. They should also be pleased with themselves for the work that they'd done, she thought.

'Everything OK now folks?' she asked.

'Yes Governor, all sorted now. I'll just need to get the orderly to give the floor a good clean tomorrow,' said the PE instructor.

'Good. Ah Fraser, I've come to see how you are; quite an ordeal then I expect?'

'Yes, I suppose so Ma'am, but it could have been a lot worse.'

'He had a weapon didn't he?' the governor asked.

'Yes, an improvised knife, nothing special,' Fraser responded.

'Yes, but enough to have caused some damage no doubt? Anyway, well done; you followed it up quickly and stayed calm, and you are OK now, those are the main things. I'm pleased,' she said with genuine feeling.

'Thanks Ma'am. Oh, and by the way, Mantel's intervention was critical. Without him, it could have been very different. If I had to wait for a full team, I don't know whether I'd be here now, to be honest. Charlie can be so volatile, he shouldn't be in prison Ma'am, secure hospital is the place for the likes of Charlie.'

'Yes, I think you are right on both counts. I'm going to see Steve Mantel next. Funny isn't it, despite all our training, it was a prisoner who played the crucial part today. There's a lesson in that, isn't there Fraser?'

'Yes Ma'am. When I worked in Cat A we had a serious assault on an officer and it was one of the prisoners who took charge and saved his life. He had been a medic in the Falklands and like Steve Mantel had skills that maybe we don't have. I've never forgotten it Ma'am.'

'Yes. Steve Mantel was a paratrooper after all, used to making quick decisions and acting in the face of danger. I'll go and see him now. Anyway Fraser, I'm glad you're OK.'

'Thanks. He's in the medical room getting cleaned up Ma'am. He got a few cuts on the razor wire while holding onto me.'

The governor reflected on her many years service and incidents that she had been involved in before. She felt proud of her staff, for today could so easily have slipped out of control and she knew from bitter experience just how nasty a full scale prison riot could be. She had worked at Strangeways during their major disturbances and it had not been pleasant. She approached the Healthcare Unit with a variety of other previous incidents going through her mind. As she entered the building Steve Mantel was already sporting quite a few plasters and bandages, razor wire being abrasive stuff.

'Steve, I didn't realise that you'd been hurt so badly, how are you feeling?' she asked.

'OK, Ma'am, it's just a few scratches. I'll be fine.'

'A real soldier, aren't you?'

'I was Ma'am. I was.'

'Well you certainly used those skills to good effect today Steve. I want to thank you, well done. I know Fraser McGregor was very impressed and relieved by your intervention. Actually both the senior fire and police officers commended you for your decisive and brave action. They both acknowledged that an official response would have been much slower and in fairness couldn't have turned out any better. Remember our conversation when we last spoke, following that incident in the visits room? Well I'm glad I kept you here and didn't send you back to Cat B. We must recognise what you did today and make sure that the Parole Board are made aware. Immediate action isn't always the best response, but it worked on this occasion. Thank you again.'

Steve felt so pleased to hear thanks and recognition for a change. He thought of Rasha and how he had let her down before, but today she could be proud of him again. He was also happy that it happened to be Fraser McGregor that he had brought down from danger. He felt that he deserved some good luck after all he had been through.

When the governor got back to the command suite to wind up the operation there was some good news. The three missing prisoners had been identified and accounted for. They had somehow managed to get out by hiding in one of the emergency vehicles, but had been picked up by the police very quickly and were now in their custody.

The area manager was on the line.

'Governor, I'm told there has been an escape; you know how seriously this will be taken?' he said sombrely.

'No, all prisoners are now accounted for Sir, no problem.'

'Ah, Margaret,' he replied in an entirely different tone, 'I understand that things have gone well overall and that ex-soldier of yours saved the day? I remember saying to you that I thought he'd come good in the end, I can usually judge these things you know. I was saying to the National Director how well Mantail had done and how he was one that I had kept a special eye on.'

'It's Mantel, Sir,' she replied.

'Yes. No matter. There will be a press conference that of course I will attend and reassure the public about their safety, and make the point that we never underestimate the people in our care and what an excellent example Mantail provided today, and how I had marked him out as different. He was an ex-Marine wasn't he?'

'An ex-paratrooper, Sir.'

'Yes, Yes. As I was saying The MOD can be proud of this one!'

She hoped so too as she put the phone down on her over ambitious, pretentious young manager.

Later Steve received an Area Manager's Commendation and Rasha was so pleased that he had managed to use his energy and skills to good effect without getting into more trouble. Anya could see some potential for influencing the Parole Board and trying to regain the lost time over the previous incident. Steve's ex-CO was delighted with his display of decisive action and felt that it would help in portraying a more positive image of him within the military.

Both Fraser McGregor and his OS Mr O'Brien had talked to him and in their own way tried to convey the same message. The message had been received and understood. Basically they had pointed out that there was something in his make up that lent itself to decisive action and that's why he had done so well in the army. Now, however, he had to learn to temper and focus that energy to be able to use it appropriately, like in helping Officer McGregor and not inappropriately like assaulting people who offended him. If he could do that, they both felt that he could have a bright future.

Chapter 12

Anya wrote with a new development. After much lobbying she had managed to persuade the MOD to release the tape of the incident in Cyprus. She had viewed it and concluded, as they had been led to believe, that the evidence was inconclusive. However she did feel that it was by no means solid enough on its own to secure a murder conviction and indeed left sufficient uncertainty that in itself would not meet the criteria of 'being beyond reasonable doubt.' None of this though was strong enough to seek an appeal without being able to cast some doubt on the crucial evidence of the bayonet, which still seemed unlikely.

Anya had found out previously that there had been other incidents of violence in which Stephan Markou had been implicated where the same type of bayonet had been used, with the implication that he used this as a deliberate tactic to distract attention away from him and on to the soldiers. However this appeared to be more hearsay than solid evidence.

She had also found out that the Royal visit cancellation was almost entirely due to strong intelligence of a terrorist threat to the Royal party and nothing to do with the aftermath of the 'murder'. Putting all this together, Anya contemplated whether it was realistic to run an appeal. On balance she concluded that it was not and that they would be better served to hold this information for the negotiations to come with the Parole Board and in attempting to secure support from the MOD for Steve's eventual release. When she next visited she explained this to Steve, who although disappointed could accept what she was saying.

Chapter 13

For the remainder of his time in Castle Gate Steve did well. He completed his two A levels, met his sentence planning targets and successfully avoided any further incidents of any kind. At work, he moved from light assembly to library orderly and later to gym orderly, where in both settings he was well thought of and demonstrated a capacity for trust and responsibility. In short, he had made the adjustment required in Cat C and was ready to face the Parole Board to seek approval for Cat D. With a ten year tariff he was still roughly on track to seek release in 2023. His studies were helping him to develop his understanding and interest in social affairs. The concepts of honesty, truth and justice still fascinated him.

Officer O'Brien explained to Steve what the process involved.

'Steve, basically the Parole Board receive reports from all concerned, including me and your offender manager, your home probation officer and have to decide whether risk has been reduced enough to warrant moving to open conditions. To do that they will want to know about your prison behaviour record, warts and all, the work that you're done and any concerns we have. As I see it I'm happy to support you on this, I think you are ready for open. It's a bit like the move from B to C, but with even more freedom and responsibility this time. OK?'

'Yes, good, I just want to get on with it and get out!' Steve replied.

So, risk assessments were updated and reports written. Mr O'Brien faithfully wrote about Steve's good behaviour, lack of adjudications and steady improvement building on the work that he had done before with Kirsty and Lucy at Farm Hill. He did of course have to mention the assault, but also made much of the rescue of Mr McGregor and the Area Manager's Commendation.

When it came to meeting his OM however, it was a different story. Rachael Mohamed had never met Steve. She had talked to Officer O'Brien and based her report on that, records and a brief telephone interview with Steve. It was difficult for him to gauge how that was going and what she thought, but he hadn't dwelt on it until he received the report, which didn't support open conditions. Steve was gutted. He felt let down by the one person who was meant to be supporting him the most.

Anya was disappointed by the contents of the report too, but felt that she could make sufficient representations to still win the day and asked if she could call both Kirsty and Lucy as additional witnesses to the hearing.

Rachael had made much of the assault on the prison officer. The fact that it was so impulsive, she argued, suggested that Steve still needed to do more work on managing his emotions and that brought up the argument about doing the CALM course again, which she recommended. She also had real reservations about his actions over intervening with Mr McGregor and argued that although it worked out OK, that it was still a very impulsive act and could have ended in tragedy. She felt that there was insufficient time or evidence to demonstrate trust and responsibility to the level required to move on. She therefore concluded that he remained too high risk and was not yet ready for Cat D.

Anya was able to reassure him at least that she could argue that the actions to help the officer were more considered than that, as evidenced by the discussions with Officer Jarrett. In the end they had to accept that the reports had been submitted and that they would have to argue it out at the hearing.

The hearing was set for two months hence and both Anya and Rasha were trying to help Steve to present himself well and to understand the process. The panel consisted of a judge as the chair and usually a psychiatrist and a senior probation manager. They would call the witnesses in turn and ask for their opinions and question their answers and reports. Steve would also be invited to speak on his own behalf and Anya could summarise the case and submit the arguments in support of Cat D on his behalf. Then the panel would go away and decide independently and submit a detailed written answer within several weeks, and their decision was final. As such it was a vital hurdle to cross and of the utmost importance that Steve was prepared and presented himself well.

On the day, obviously Steve felt quite nervous. He couldn't help compare it to the military process and the sentencing court in Cyprus. Anya tried to reassure him that this would be less formal and more relaxed. Nevertheless, again he found himself in a position where others would decide on the course of his life and he could only play a small part in that process. He was given a brief chance to speak to Anya in private first and to see both Kirsty and Lucy again. They were pleased to hear how he was getting on.

Then they were all called in. The room was relatively small and the panel didn't look too intimidating. Mr O'Brien was asked to speak first.

He outlined his report and concluded; 'I'm only a prison officer, Sir, I haven't got degrees or the like, but I've been doing this job for a long time and I reckon I'm a pretty good judge of character and this lad strikes me as sound. He's always been honest with me, including about his mistakes, and there have been examples of him considering situations for some time before doing anything. He has a very strong sense of right and wrong and is prepared to defend it and I admire him for that. I don't readily recommend progression and am known for being firm and am considered by some to be too harsh, so for me this is unusual.'

'So you think he is ready for open conditions?' asked the judge.

'Yes, Sir, I do,' he replied firmly.

'Can you inform us how as a prisoner Mr Mantel managed to expedite such a rescue as he did?'

Mr O'Brien described the circumstances of the whole event to their satisfaction, before the judge invited the other panel members to ask questions.

The psychiatrist probed around the issue of how far Steve had learnt about his make up, when it was best to act instinctively and when it was better to be more considered. He questioned how far Steve appreciated the differences between military and civilian life and how far he had actually learnt to manage his emotions.

Other witnesses took their turn and Rachael Mohamed attracted the greatest range of questions.

The probation senior manager questioned her experience and how she could reasonably offer such a firm assessment having never met the man. She did however seem to share some of her misgivings.

Kirsty and Lucy spoke with conviction about Steve's work and progress, which did seem to impress the panel.

When eventually it came to Steve's turn he was feeling somewhat jaded by the experience, trying to concentrate and read which way it was going; he wondered if they were being persuaded in his favour. Now he had to perform, and perform he did. He knew that Rasha would have accepted nothing less. He was invited to explain in his own words why he thought he was ready for open conditions.

'Sir, I suppose it rests on what I did, what I think I've learned and would I do it differently another time.'

'Go on,' encouraged the judge.

'I accept now, Sir, that I was holding the bayonet when it penetrated the victim's chest and killed him, although I still maintain that there was another gloved hand on that weapon and despite the whole thing being foolhardy, I never set out with the intention of killing anyone.

I was a soldier, Sir, I had been trained to fight, I thought that I was fighting for justice Sir, but found that war can be so devastatingly random and is often unjust. In the immediate period after fighting in Afghanistan, when I arrived in Cyprus I thought that I had left all that deceit behind, but became aware of a whole pattern of serious injustice and I condemned it utterly and still do. The mistake I made, Sir, and this also applies to assaulting the officer, was to act in the wrong way and to act before I had thought it through. I could have done it differently. If I'd have done that, perhaps people would not have got hurt and I wouldn't be here now, Sir. Would I do it differently again?   I sincerely hope so.'

The room was silent listening to Steve's words when the judge challenged him further.

'So, Mr Mantel, how would you approach something like this again?'

'I hope I would still have the courage to see injustice, Sir, but I have to accept that my powers and responsibilities are limited. In future I would need to find out who are the right people to tell and to leave it to them, but I really hope that I would never ignore it.'

After Anya delivered her summing up and the judge had explained the next steps, the hearing was over and the panel retired to their deliberations. People came up to Steve and generally commented that they thought that he had come across well and that the hearing had also gone well in general. He felt relieved. Anya felt that they had certainly made their case.

In the retiring room the panel resumed the serious task of taking an independent view of the risks and benefits of sanctioning open conditions. The judge summarised the evidence as he saw it and asked his colleagues for their overview. The probation senior manager on balance felt that the case had been made for progression and that the risks were clear and manageable. The psychiatrist however was more sceptical.

'My problem is that he is still a young man and one full of hormones and energy and that he is imbued in a culture of immediate action. I consider that for many years yet, if he was challenged in a way that pushed some of those buttons, he would find it very difficult to do other than react, and that could be a problem.'

They debated the point at some length.

'But at the end of the day, has he done enough to satisfy us that it is on balance safe and manageable to move him to open conditions where we can test out his reactions with reasonable control?' posed the judge.

'Yes, put like that, I believe so. In his favour I believe him when he says that he did not set out to kill anyone. He was a soldier, he had nothing to prove. Some of his views are admiral, as are some of his actions. We just need to help him channel them in the right direction,' replied the psychiatrist.

'There aren't any specific victim considerations here, are there?' posed the judge.

'No, in fact little is known about the man who died. Apparently he was an illegal immigrant recruited by Stephan Markou. He had no family and indeed his identity and his name for example were never fully established.'

'OK, and Markou has since been discredited and the situation in Cyprus has moved on,' summarised the judge. 'So, are we all happy?' to which there were nods.

'So, we are agreed to sanction open conditions. I shall write up our response and seek to get it back to the prison quickly. An interesting case, would you prefer to log this on for us to hear the follow up, assuming he does apply for release at the first available opportunity?'

'Yes,' they were all agreed.

For Rasha, Anya and Steve the following few weeks were really tense, waiting to hear from the Parole Board. Steve tried to just focus on day to day matters and the others were busy. It was probably most difficult for Rasha, partly because she had not been present at the hearing to form her own view on Steve's chances of success, but also because she was so desperate for it to work out for them. When the letter came, Anya actually received her letter first before the prison informed Steve and gave him his copy. So by the time he rang her, Rasha had already cried several buckets of tears of joy and relief. She sounded so excited on the phone. This actually meant home leave and private time together, not behind a glass screen or in a busy visits hall, but together on their own, in a home environment, and the opportunity to be intimate. How good would that be, she thought?

Both Officer McGregor and O'Brien were quick to offer their good wishes and Steve felt some real momentum. Maybe now he could dare to dream about an open door? He too looked forward to time with Rasha, alone, in bed, anywhere! How odd it felt to be in love with a women who he had never been alone with since their first meeting in that dark, dingy, filthy, disgusting brothel. How odd. How would it feel? How long would he have to wait?

In discussions with Officer O'Brien, Steve remembered Rasha's words of advice and he asked to be considered for HMP Bardon Wood, the nearest Cat D to Rasha. In the end, it was considered unsuitable; places were limited and it seemed likely to be earmarked for closure as government had moved away from separate Cat D prisons so he wasn't too disappointed, but the alternative was HMP Southdown, south of London, nearer the coast. This was a Cat C with a distinct, separate Cat D resettlement unit. It did offer a good reputation for community work projects. Steve was also given a series of key dates including when he could start home leaves. It wasn't too far away. They spoke to his OM on a conference phone who by now was a different supervisor and as Steve was targeting London for release, negotiations to transfer his case were also under way, which would mean yet another change of probation officer.

In the end, it all came at once with a move, a new London based OM in the patch where Rasha lived and the prospect of a first home leave to her flat.

Chapter 14

Steve got off the train and felt bemused and somewhat overwhelmed by the number of people milling around at the station. He was waiting pensively. Then he saw her. Rasha was running towards him with arms outstretched. Steve dropped his bags and flung open his arms to envelope her as she reached him. They touched and their lips met. After a long, loving kiss and embrace, they moved off holding hands, with Rasha talking at great pace about all the plans that she had made; the meal she was going to cook tonight in the flat, through visits to various places, shopping and walking by the river, all interspersed, she hoped, by frequent love-making.

She guided him by hand through the crowds to a taxi rank. They sat in the back seat and cuddled, while Rasha called out her address. The taxi driver had seen it all before.

'Back from leave, mate? I can see she's pleased to see you!'

Steve could almost imagine that this was just after Cyprus, not years later.

'Yes, something like that, mate,' he replied.

They got out at her flat and Steve just felt overwhelmed. He was looking at his potential new home. He'd never been here before and after all the waiting he stood in front the block of flats with the woman of his dreams by his side.

'Come on,' she said, 'let's go inside!'

Steve responded and being a romantic carried her through the door and into unfamiliar territory. He was immediately impressed. Although the flat had a 'girlie' feel to it, he could also recognise her subtle touches at trying to introduce elements of masculinity. As he walked through the rooms, he came across a corner display of some of his old military kit. It must have been the stuff from Cyprus; his beret, a few bits and pieces and some photographs. It was then that he realised that they had no photographs of each other together. He wondered if Rasha had a camera.

She just stood looking at him, as he took it all in, admiring him, wanting him. She was so pleased by his reaction. She wanted him to feel that this was a part of him, too. Steve felt a real sense of appreciation that he was so lucky to have someone supporting him like this, when most other prisoners that he had talked to had nothing and no one. The thought however soon passed with a rush of emotion that at last they were together, alone.

They embraced and gazed into each other's eyes. It felt so right and they both felt so ready. They had waited so long. Their patience was soon to be rewarded. Rasha smiled acknowledging that it was time, walking towards the bedroom, beckoning him, starting to undress, starting to prepare, yearning, longing.

They made love with a vigour, an intensity and a passion that reflected their journey together. It had been a special moment. They lay naked next to each other in bed for sometime, laughing, loving, exploring. It felt unreal, a dream. Steve soon suggested a second attempt, 'For quality control reasons'. Rasha laughed and replied, 'You'll be saying next that it is being recorded for training and audit purposes!' Laughter ensued again until passion overtook them and they fell away to relax and to sleep awhile, together.

Chapter 15

Southdown proved to be another massive adjustment for Steve. It was a small unit, with few staff, a relaxed atmosphere and a far greater sense of freedom and responsibility than he had been used to. He was allocated to an adventure training project for deprived children and loved the opportunity to be outside and active again. The kids readily related to him and he did well, using his military skills to challenge them in physical pursuits and in building simple obstacle courses and challenges using ropes and climbing techniques. Steve fitted in well and his CO was also pleased that he could get some experience of doing something relevant to fit with his plans for employment on release.

After a period of adjustment, Steve enjoyed rekindling his sense of personal motivation to get himself up and ready in the morning, to leave the prison and travel to work on a daily basis independently. The time went much quicker and he had regular home leave to look forward to as well. He found that he could relate to both his probation officers inside the prison and in his home area. Resettlement plans were coming together well to be able to work with his ex-CO and live with Rasha. Special permission was being sought to vary his licence to allow for work away and work abroad. Traditionally this had not been possible but a change in the regulations in 2018 acknowledged that to facilitate resettlement in an evermore international world, arrangements for licence needed to be more flexible, and agreements were being reached to share information across national boundaries and start reciprocal arrangements for supervision. Alongside developments in greater cooperation in detecting crime across borders, this made a lot of sense.

Steve anticipated two more years in Cat D before the prospect of returning to the Parole Board to apply for release by 2023, having served his ten year minimum tariff.

Cat D was an interesting experience. Steve had heard stories of drink, drugs, women and parties being common place with staffing levels so low and most people working outside the prison. He certainly was aware of the availability of booze and even the odd take-away, but hadn't seen any parties. He did manage to discipline himself to avoid this sort of thing as every so often the authorities swooped down and people were caught and shipped back to closed conditions. He knew that if he allowed that to happen it could delay his release for about five years. He couldn't bear the thought of that, or of Rasha's reaction. He simply couldn't do that to her.

The best stories were of brothers or identical twins exchanging places over the weekends to allow the prisoner to get out. He wasn't sure if it was true, but he had certainly heard it spoken of several times. The closest he came to disaster himself was getting involved with another prisoner, another ex-soldier who eventually got arrested for a suspected armed robbery committed in his area whilst he was on home leave. Steve never saw him again.

Steve was due to meet with both probation officers the following day to confirm future plans, and he was thinking about what to say as he travelled back to the prison from work on the bus. One thing he wanted to raise was the problems with securing grants if he wanted to do a degree course. He was in two minds whether to do further NVQs or whether his old CO would really be bothered if he had more qualifications or not. The CO was also invited to help coordinate arrangements. Steve was also interested to know how he was perceived to be getting on and how his application for the licence variation was going.

The following morning Steve stayed off work to meet the appointment. He took the opportunity to write to Rasha. Steve felt so glad that she had maintained faith in him. He felt so lucky and frequently thought back to their moments together, of making love, of holding hands, of planning and dreaming. He now had so much to live for, so much to look forward too.

He walked over to the gate to meet his visitors feeling relaxed.

'Morning, gents,' he called out as he entered the room. The others had made their introductions and were chatting comfortably.

'Sit down, Steve; how are you?' asked Craig Rutherford his OM.

'I'm fine thanks, Craig. Enjoying Cat D,' he replied.

'Good, so what about future plans then guys?' posed Lee Lamont his OS.

'Well, things have gone well with home leave arrangements. I've met Rasha and have to report how comfortable they look together. I have no concerns there. He's also working well on the adventure training project he tells me, said Craig.

'Yes, he is. Both the staff at the project and the kids love him,' replied Lee, 'and I gather you still hope to offer him a job, Lance?' he asked the ex-CO.

'Yes, I do. My business is going well and there will be an opening there. The army are also warming to his progress and there are no issues coming out of Cyprus that I am aware of, so I'm all ready to go, as soon as you let him out,' Lance replied, smiling at Steve.

'Any concerns or questions from you, Steve? I remember that you were keen to confirm that your licence will be varied as we discussed, and that is all going through,' added Craig.

'That's good,' replied Steve. 'I also wondered about what you think about taking further qualifications? I reckon I want to develop the adventure training side and perhaps then go into journalism as I get older.'

'Sounds good,' said Lance.

They agreed that Steve was progressing well. There had been no reoccurrence of impetuous or violent behaviour, indeed there were plenty of examples of positive thinking and mature responses. Release plans were firming up comprehensively and there seemed to be no significant obstacles left to navigate. All the messages were that if Steve could maintain current performance there should be no problem in convincing the Parole Board that he was ready for release.

Chapter 16

Steve was walking through the streets of London towards Rasha's flat on his second home leave when a car pulled up along side him and two big guys bundled him into the back seat. They drove off in silence at high speed. Steve didn't recognise them and wasn't sure what was going on. All the men in the car were of oriental origin. Steve wondered, what was that about? They raced through the streets, turning frequently. He hadn't got a clue where he was.

The car turned into an industrial estate and as they approached a particular unit, a rolling door opened and they drove in. Steve was invited to get out of the car. He faced a line of more oriental men dressed in dark suits with a man in the middle who stepped forward.

'Welcome, Mr Mantel. My name is B3. It was us who eliminated Stephan Markou in Cyprus, he got greedy. We were grateful to you then for pointing out his treachery. We were disappointed however that you failed to kill him at the time. No matter now. We are aware that you are shortly due for release and wanted to make our terms clear. So here's the deal…and remember we could kill you at any time, and your beautiful partner if we choose.'

Steve could feel his hackles rising. Threaten him by all means, but not Rasha.

'This is about me, leave her out of it,' he replied.

'You are in no position to negotiate. As I was saying... we want your reassurance that you have no further interest in Cyprus, and you can keep the boy by the way.'

'You have it,' Steve replied, thinking of Ben.

'If you honour it, we will leave you alone... And one more thing...we may want a favour; a man with your skills could be useful to us...if we had to eliminate someone here in London.'

Steve felt cold; how could he live with that? he thought.

'You may go now, but just to ensure you know where you stand we will leave you with this,' said B3 as two of his men moved forward quickly, cut him on the side of his face, hooded and bound him and bundled him back into the car, this time in the boot. They set off again. Steve was quickly disorientated and confused. Different thoughts rushed through his mind.

The car stopped and the boot opened. He was untied and the hood was removed. Before he could adjust, the car was gone and he was alone in a quiet side street somewhere, anywhere in London with what he stood up in and with a cut on his face. What now he thought? Should I ring the police, ring Rasha, ring Anya? No, he thought, best not; first I need to clean up and then think. He looked around him. He had no idea where he was. There were no obvious reference points within sight. A taxi approached and he took his chance and signalled to the driver and got in.

'You alright, mate? Been roughed up a bit?' he asked.

'Yeah,' said Steve, 'just been jumped for my wallet, but I got away. Can you take me to a decent café where I can clean up and just sit for a while?'

'Yeah, sure mate,' said the driver as he drove along a few streets, stopped, wished him well and let him out with no charge.

Rasha was getting worried. What had happened, she thought, he should be here by now? She rang him, but his phone was switched off.

Steve put his sleeve to his face, ordered a coffee and went into the toilet to sort himself out. The cut was quite deep, they wanted it to scar he guessed. It was about two inches long and just off the side of his face, up by his eye. As he emerged a waitress appeared, he guessed she was Eastern European. She spoke quietly and sat him down and applied some plaster strips and a gauze patch. Maybe this was common place around here? He didn't know and he didn't ask. He just thanked her and went to drink his coffee.

What now? he thought.

Calmly, Steve considered his options. What to do, who to turn to? He thought long and hard and decided that his best option, of course, was to contact his CO. There, he had a plan! He rang...

'Sir, its Steve, I'm in London and in a spot of trouble, I could do with your help…'

'OK,' Lance replied.

Steve explained what had happened, standing outside the back of the café out of ear shot and that really he needed stitches but didn't want to report to a hospital. Lance immediately understood and was actually in London with some of his team, including his medic, who could easily sort this out, so they arranged to meet. Steve felt reassured, that was the immediate problem dealt with…he thought his psychologist would have been proud of him. Better ring Rasha next…

'Rasha, it's me. Sorry, something has come up, I'll be late, but don't worry I'll explain later.'

'Steve, what's wrong! I was really concerned,' she replied.

'Don't worry, it's nothing.'

'Don't lie to me, I can tell! What's wrong?'

'You'll have to trust me; I'll get to you as soon as I can,' and he rang off.

Rasha would wait, but she would also worry.

Steve met up with Lance and his team and they soon stitched up his face.

'Quite a designer scar that will be,' said his medic.

Lance could see the implications of this development with the involvement of a Chinese gang, this changed everything. They talked and chewed it over thoroughly before deciding what they should do. Steve was grateful. He felt that he had made the right choice. Sentence planning could score this one for him!

'Right, come on, a pint!' said Lance.

'No Sir, I can't. Licence conditions, no pubs, no booze or drugs. Honestly! I can't risk it.'

'OK, anyway, you had better be off to that woman of yours and I think its time to drop the Sir, we are both civilians now; it's Lance. How are you going to handle this Steve, you'll have to tell the authorities?'

'Yes you are right, I'd better go...Lance.' It felt so odd calling his ex-CO by his first name. Steve set off smartly having got his bearings towards the nearest tube station. After several stops he approached Rasha's flat and as he opened the door, she threw her arms around him and burst into tears.

'What went wrong, Steve? You must tell me everything. You must never lie to me. We haven't gone through all this to have secrets,' she said through tears.

Steve realised that he had hurt her feelings. He would never want to hurt her. He apologised and explained most of the story.

Rasha wanted to bathe his wound, but he assured her that it would be OK. He warned that he would need to keep in touch with Lance over the weekend. He felt that this would spoil the leave, but it was, he supposed, their first test together.

Rasha felt deeply worried, but served some food nevertheless. They ate quietly, somewhat subdued.

Later in bed after rekindling their passion for each other, Rasha snuggled up against Steve and asked 'What are you going to do?'

'Would you mind if I ask Lance to join us tomorrow?' he asked tentatively.

'No, of course not, if you think it will help.'

'Well then, let's do that and plan in more detail. We will need to add some security to the flat. I will have to tell the prison authorities and this will affect plans for release, Rasha.'

'Are you saying they won't let you out?'

'No, just that it will be more complicated, but I think not to tell them would make it worse. If nothing else, they won't believe me if I say I picked up this cut walking into a cupboard!'

The following morning they sat down with Lance for coffee in the flat. He agreed about the security and offered to see to it. You'll need some quality locks, a spy hole, a reliable mobile phone. Have my number, Rasha, report any concerns any time of day or night. You'll also need a link with the authorities if necessary and later maybe even a secure room.'

'What do you think I should do about their threat to lean on me to work for them, Sir...I mean Lance?' Steve asked whilst Rasha was in the kitchen.

'Um, that is the difficult one. You don't need to have any connection with Cyprus, but leaning on you here is a different dimension that you really don't need. I'll speak to military intelligence and we may have to involve MI5 and MI6 in this.'

'That serious?'

'Yes, I think so. Implications for international crime or terrorism on the streets of London, and involvement of a convicted murderer on life licence, who is an ex-soldier - I should say so!' he replied as Rasha returned.

'I was just saying, Rasha, what a lucky man he is and how good you appear together.'

Rasha smiled, taking the praise but knowing it was offered as a swift way of changing the subject.

Lance agreed to make further enquiries and left them alone.

Rasha came up close again. 'We will be alright Steve, won't we? she asked lovingly.

'Yes, of course. I'd do anything to protect you, you know that don't you?'

'Yes, I do, and that's what worries me,' she replied soberly.

The weekend ended in fairly serious mood given the change in circumstances and Steve really didn't want to leave her and return to the prison to face the music, but knew that he had to.

****

At the gate the officer saw him coming in. 'Cut yourself shaving, Steve?' he gibed.

'Something like that!' he replied.

Steve knew the officer and asked, 'Are you on duty tomorrow, Sir?'

'Yes, I'll be here.'

'I'll need to see the lifer manager urgently. Can you fix it for me?'

'OK. Trouble?'

'Yes, I'm afraid so,' replied Steve as he walked on towards his bunk. He dumped his kit and lay on the bed wondering if this nightmare would ever end and he'd be truly free to get on with his life. He felt for Rasha, she had been through so much, and now this.

In the morning the lifer manager responded. 'Mantel, I gather you need to see me? What happened to your face incidentally?'

Steve explained the full story; the kidnap, the wound and his considerations with Lance.

'I see,' said his lifer manager. 'You realise this is serious and that this changes everything?'

'Yes, I'm afraid I think I do.'

'OK. I'll need to talk to your Lance and our police liaison officer. Do you want to get healthcare to look at that cut? Did you report all this at all?'

'To the local police, you mean?'

'Precisely.'

'No. I didn't think reporting it as a crime straight away would help. The London police probably wouldn't have believed me and I could have been bundled straight back to the nearest prison, spoiled my weekend and left me potentially back in closed conditions. Not a good plan eh?'

'Yeah, OK, you're probably right. Well, best just lay low for a couple of days while I make enquiries and we'll see where we go from here, but well done for reporting it, at least that says something.'

'OK, Sir. Thanks,' said Steve recognising that the lifer manager was a reasonable bloke.

The lifer manager went straight to see the governor who was a very experienced old bruiser, keen to keep a stable ship and avoid any high profile risks for the local community. He briefed him succinctly.

'Um, we might have to shunt him back into closed while we sort this out. Let's at least put him in the Seg straight away for his own protection until we knew exactly who these guys are. When you've done that let's get that Lance on the conference phone with a police link.'

'Will do, Sir!'

He explained to Steve the governor's decision and went on to contact the other people the governor had mentioned. Steve was gutted but understood. This was the sort of reaction he feared and had hoped to avoid. He feared being sent all the way back to Cat B and being left there to rot.

Lance had quickly got things moving. Calls rushed around London police HQ intelligence community including contacts with MI5 and 6.

By mid morning a conference video link was all set up between the governor, the local chief constable, a metropolitan police assistant chief constable, a rep from MI5 and 6, Lance and the lifer manager.

'Morning, Gentlemen,' the governor opened, 'thank you all for responding so quickly and making yourselves available. Ross here, the lifer manager, will take a note.' Introductions were made and absolute confidentiality confirmed.

'So, Gentlemen, what have we got?'

The ACC responded first. 'This is serious. We know B3 and the criminal group he represents. They are one of China's leading criminal organisations, reputedly with some very high connections. They kill without conscience to protect their empire and on behalf of government when it suits. If they seriously thought your prisoner was a threat to their operations in Cyprus they would have killed him yesterday, no doubt. So they don't. As to using him to do their dirty work over here, yes they would, and if he wasn't keen they would persuade him.'

'Meaning what, exactly?' asked the chief constable.

'Firing Rasha's flat, the whole block with her and anyone else in it, for example.'

Turning to the MI5 and 6 representatives who had only introduced themselves as such, the governor asked them for their take on the situation.

'B3 represents a serious threat to the interests of this country, both at home and abroad. We want him out of the game, but there is politics involved.'

'If you could entrap him, would Steve Mantel potentially play a part in that?' asked the governor.

'No,' replied the man from MI6, 'but he could get in the way.'

'And what would that mean?' asked Lance.

'He'd be expendable.'

'And what's the government line on this? I don't want any embarrassment to the criminal justice system or anything to reflect badly on the prison,' responded the governor.

'From an intelligence point of view, we don't care about those considerations, they don't feature. I'm just being honest with you, if there is a chance to nail B3 your man won't be a consideration I assure you.'

Silence covered the room while they all considered the implications. Lance spoke first.

'Remember, Gentlemen, there is a young man caught up in this who has no connection with politics, terrorism or criminal gangs. I see the wider picture, but I feel for him, he's suffered enough for wider causes and I want to see him thrive because he still has so much more to give.'

'Honourable sentiment maybe, but he did murder someone. I can't be sentimental,' said the ACC.

'You may call it sentiment, ACC, but in the military we call it loyalty.'

'So what would you suggest, Colonel?'

'You obviously need to keep tabs on this Chinese gang, but you've made it clear that Steve Mantel is no consideration in this and I don't think it should derail his plans. I think we need to push for his licence variation so that I can keep him employed and out of the spotlight, and it sounds like you need to take the threat to Rasha and that whole block of flats seriously ACC.'

'Yes, I assure you I will,' replied the ACC.

'OK, thank you, Gentlemen. So we'll carry on. If we know about any further attempts to use Mantel by these people we will be in touch, directly to you ACC?' said the governor. The ACC nodded.

'We'll arrange for a handler to make contact with Mantel once released and make it plain to him that he is to contact him directly and immediately if any concerns arise. OK, MI5, with you?' to further nods, 'I don't think we need to disseminate this information any further down the line at this stage, the tighter the group who knows the better.'

The conference closed and the members departed swiftly. The governor took a deep breath and turned to Ross, 'You got that?'

'Yes, I think so, Sir; if Steve Mantel happens to get caught up in this the system will hang him out to dry if the gang don't kill him first, and if there's any flack associated with criminal justice we are on our own.'

'Yes, that's about it,' concluded the governor.

Chapter 17

Steve's licence variation was expedited swiftly. He was kept on site for the rest of the week until the governor and the local chief constable had agreed that the immediate threat to the community, the prison or to him was negligible. MI5 agreed to take the liaison lead and keep them informed if there was any reason to believe the threat was raised, otherwise it was agreed that Steve's home leaves could continue as normal, but if necessary could be pulled immediately. Given the profile of this affair, a core group was formed of those attending the video conference and controlled very tightly on a need to know basis, and London MAPPA were briefed. Given the nature of the capital city, arrangements for the coordination of public protection were unique. MAPPA; Multi Agency Public Protection Arrangements, enshrined in legislation since 2000 had the onerous task of coordinating plans for high risk and high profile prison releases, including at times terrorism connections and deportation. The extra dimension of a core group in this case was a complication but in comparison with many London cases this matter was regarded as relatively routine.

The following week Steve was back at the project and feeling very relieved not to have been moved back to Cat B, so of course was Rasha and incidentally Lance. Things settled down again, Steve was deemed to be progressing well and had several further home leaves without incident. His love for Rasha was deepening and they were managing the adjustment well to their new circumstances. Partings were always painful, but greetings were so exciting. They both looked forward to a greater sense of permanency. Steve also thought of the potential freedom inherent on expeditions with Lance.

Time was approaching the end of his ten year tariff and a meeting had been called to consider the implications. Lee Lamont, Steve's OS had linked up with Craig Rutherford the OM based in London by video conference. Ross, the lifer manager opened the meeting.

'Morning to you all. Today we meet to discuss Steve's progress and decide whether we are satisfied to recommend release at the forthcoming oral hearing with the Parole Board and any implication for resettlement or licence conditions. So Lee, can you summarise progress from the prison perspective?'

'Yes, it's all good. Steve has responded well to open conditions, there have been no discipline concerns, work reports are good from outside and his home leaves have gone well, giving us some confidence about his release plan. He also has good prospects for employment with Lance, his ex-CO. There is also ample evidence to suggest greater reflection and more considered actions, rather than being impetuous, which has got him into trouble before. The only issue really has been the concern about any potential rekindling of connections with Cyprus.'

Those present were not all fully aware of what that meant, but knew that there was some risk of criminal association.

'And you Craig?' asked the lifer manager.

'Yes, I've been impressed too. The strength and resilience of Steve and Rasha's relationship is impressive, not many prisoners sustain relationships through this length of time. All in all I'm happy to support release and will be writing my report to that effect. As regards licence conditions, apart from the usual ones, we could include a condition to inform his OM if the criminal associates from Cyprus attempt to contact him?'

They agreed that would be helpful.

'Steve, anything from you?' asked Ross.

'No Sir, I'm happy with all of that, I just want to go now, Sir. It's been a long time.'

'OK then gents, my only reservation at this stage is the wider security picture and how the Parole Board may regard that. They will want to be assured about MAPPA plans Craig, so please make sure you include that in your report. But let's not forget the progress Steve has made and the key changes in his decision making. He is now far more considered and far less impulsive and that for me bodes well, so well done!'

Chapter 18

On the day of the hearing Steve felt understandably tense. He reflected back on his ten years. He felt genuinely sorry that the guy had died, but still mostly blamed Markou for that. He felt some pride in how far he had come, a longing for Rasha and some apprehension about B3 and the Chinese connection.

It was good to see Anya again, it had been a while. She said how pleased she was about how things had worked out between him and Rasha and that Ben was doing well in school and was talking about wanting to join the army as an officer. Steve felt so pleased for him and so proud. It reminded him that some good had come out of all of this mess; he had still saved a boy's life.

As they had suggested, the same panel reconvened to hear this second application, this time not for open conditions, but for release. Evidence was taken from all the key players. Both the OM and the OS spoke up well in support. The secretary of state's representations were presented in suitably guarded terms about the wider risks of becoming embroiled in criminal activity again.

Steve thought that probably more had been said to the panel behind closed doors and he just hoped that they were suitably reassured by arrangements in place with MAPPA and liaison with the Met and MI5.

When it came to his turn, he tried to sound confident and convincing, without pleading, and thought that he'd done OK, but it was down to Anya to really bring the case home, and she did.

'In summing up, I remind you of the original circumstances of the offence and the context in which it was committed. Since then Steve Mantel has addressed himself to the task of rehabilitation with due diligence. He has progressed well through the system, demonstrating trust and responsibility time and time again and most significantly has developed his thinking and decision making. Recent events indicate a man who now weighs up situations carefully and makes considered decisions, which is a major shift and a significant development. I also remind you that this is his first and only criminal conviction. There is no pattern of criminal behaviour here. Resettlement and support arrangements are comprehensive and have been extensively tested. On that basis I hope that the panel will feel sufficiently reassured to sanction release at this point in his sentence. He would of course remain on life licence and is fully aware of the implications of that responsibility.'

The panel retired having promised to report back promptly in writing with their deliberations. The psychiatrist who had the greatest reservations last time was more reassured, 'You have to hand it to the guy, he has made remarkable progress,' he commented as they sat down. After some discussion their possession was agreed with the reservations about early warning and prompt actions if there were any indications of deterioration made explicit.

After a tense few weeks, the letter came. It carefully outlined Steve's progress against identified risks, safeguards in place and on balance concluded that risk had been sufficiently reduced and could now be safely managed in the community and therefore that release was approved.

After a few more hurdles of officialdom, a date was set and on 1st April 2024, just over ten years after being sentenced, a front gate was opened and an excited Steve Mantel walked through it to freedom, armed with a few tatty possessions, a humble discharge grant, a rail warrant and a bag full of hopes and dreams.

****

PART TWO

Chapter 19

Steve walked out into UK 2024 to discover that many things had changed.

Jeremy Hunt led a minority Tory government, Scotland had stayed in the UK and we had entered the euro zone, controversially abandoning the pound. Developments in energy efficiency had come on leaps and bounds, with many off shore energy farms generating power from blocks of new generation wind turbines with wave energy tunnels beneath them. Cars had become much more efficient with the latest generation of petrol engines routinely yielding 100 MPG and battery life extending to ranges in excess of 500 miles before recharging at one of the many accessible charging points. Early growth in the use of robots was encouraging. Valuable infrastructure projects were oft talked about as a means to promote economic growth but seldom funded, and HS2, the north-south rail link had long since been abandoned as too expensive.

Climate change had proved not to be as critical as first feared and the world had improved its capacity to respond to international crisis' and natural disasters through a well coordinated

United National Relief Agency. China was taking tentative steps towards greater liberalisation and starting to play more of a lead role in international affairs, after they had been persuaded to provide the majority of troops to fight the first Iran war in 2017.

For Steve, emerging from prison back into the world outside it was the pace of change in technology that struck him most. The rapid spread of the use of mobile phones and computer devices and the greater use of technology in so many different fields; seeing virtually everybody walking the streets fixated by the device in their hand seemed really odd to the point of being surreal. Didn't people look at each other anymore, he wondered?

Steve and Rasha settled quickly into their new routine with a wave of enthusiasm. Ben spent time with them in school holidays and was hoping to go to university to study International Relations. He had ambitions to join the army as an officer in the Parachute Regiment. The MOD in the face of fierce resistance was trying to gain support for a radical plan to transform British Forces and deliver considerable savings. It involved amalgamating all three services under one lead and rationalising all training and support services as Combined British Forces, CBF, and disbanding the separate army, navy and air force. If this was to happen it was likely that Ben would be affected and train in a combined officer training facility and hopefully would join a united single elite forces formation.

Jokes were circulating about green and red striped berets representing the old Marine and Para colours and sailors being expected to drive tanks and gunners fly aircraft!

Steve got on well with Craig, his probation officer. The probation service had expanded with better links and combined operations with other key services. The ill conceived attempt at privatisation had failed and all statutory offender supervision had returned to the public sector. Long term licence arrangements had become far more flexible and Steve was benefiting from the opportunity to negotiate clear expectations that allowed for some travel associated with his job with Lance.

Arrangements were also well ahead to radically reduce the prison population and shift resources into community provision. The women's prisons estate had been reduced to only three national establishments concentrating only on high risk offenders with all others being dealt with in their local areas in small community based Women's Centres. The main driver had been cost, as the weight of international research evidence cast severe doubt on the long held assertion that locking up ever greater numbers subject to ever longer sentences really did protect the public at a sustainable and justifiable cost.

Work with Lance was going well. Steve enjoyed the freedom so much and was getting on well with the team. They were forming a long range patrol group that would have the capacity to parachute into areas where transport infrastructure had been disrupted following a natural disaster and offer first aid, help with building improvised shelters and general survival and disaster relief. Lance had been delighted when he had won the contract to provide this service for the UN, on call 24/7 at short notice to move. The team were forming up well under Lance's leadership with potentially two ex-Paras, one ex-Marine Captain, two ex-Ghurkhas soldiers, two experienced Australian climbers and an ex-SAS Sergeant. Lance and Steve were the Paras offering their traditional toughness in adversity and determination, the Marine Captain particularly for his boat experience, the Ghurkhas for their jungle and mountain knowledge, the climbers to fill that gap and the SAS man for survival and medical skills. It was forming up as a strong team. One of the Ghurkhas was also an experienced signaller.

They started with relatively low level familiarisation and team training in Scotland. Steve loved the challenge and getting back to the rugged outdoor life. On their first trip Lance had organised some basic boat training with embarkation and disembarkation drills at speed and training up potential drivers, some survival techniques, basic navigation practice and some rope work. They were getting into shape. Of course Lance couldn't predict if and when they would be called upon by the UN, but all of this preparation was also useful for the business in general. Their next booking was with a private high profile school to lead an adventure training and expedition package in the same part of Scotland. The combination of scope for water activity with both the lochs and the sea together with spectacular mountains and of course the potentially challenging weather was judged to be ideal, as against a sunshine jolly abroad. Many of the potential candidates for the experience were already looking to join the military and this was a useful pre selection.

They formed up on the school rugby pitches with all their kit. The school were well prepared. A few favours had been called in and arms twisted as a good potential recruitment exercise to secure the use of one of the force's new generation of Chinook helicopters on route to a legitimate military exercise in Scotland. It was diverted to collect the whole party and all their equipment in one lift.

The boys were really excited as they took off and flew away. The school was used to developing leadership skills and put a significant emphasis on competitive sport. Eight man teams were already in place with dedicated leaders. They flew over the central ridge of England and on up into the highlands, eventually landing at a pre-arranged remote location. Some of Lance's team had travelled up with the party and the remainder were on site to greet them on arrival.

The teams were quickly moved off the helicopter and formed up in a forest clearing. They were then briefed for an immediate high speed boat journey across the loch and onto the far side, where a twenty mile trek awaited them to reach their isolated base camp.

On arrival they were all pretty knackered, not only by the distance but also by the terrain, and indeed as the school had hoped, nature played its part too by providing cold conditions and driving rain. The ten day event however proved to be a great success from several angles. The school got what they wanted; a tough challenge, the participants all felt that they had benefited from it and Lance's team had used the opportunity to shake out and start to bond. It had gone well, even for the one young man who had fallen during abseiling and broken his arm.

Steve needed to report into Craig at the first opportunity on completion, once the group had moved off this time by coach. Lance spoke to him to verify his location and Craig was happy.

'What's next Lance? What else have you got lined up?

'We do need some jungle training and I have an important corporate customer who wants a jungle experience, so we can combine the two,' Lance replied.

Steve was so excited and so glad to be included. As probably the least experienced member of the group he was almost the tea boy, but accepted the ribbing in good grace.

'OK Mantel, back to your cell now!' cried Sandy McGill, the ex-SAS Sergeant.

'Piss off!' he replied politely.

'Come on, no more idling about courtesy of Her Majesty, pull your finger out and get all that kit packed away and maybe I'll let you off today's flogging.'

'Oh, you are so gracious, oh wonderful master,' Steve grovelled in reply.

The team stayed on one more night for debriefing and teambuilding including a good session in the hitherto small quiet local. It felt good for Steve to be relaxed enough to let his hair down, although the team kept ribbing him by threatening to report him to his probation officer.

On the return journey by coach, he slept and thought of Rasha. He was looking forward to seeing her again. With the difficulties of poor mobile signals in the mountains this was the longest he'd gone without speaking to her for a long time. As the coach rumbled on and morning approached he rang just to make sure that she was alright. Thankfully she was. Steve was grateful to Lance for arranging to up the level of security on the flat, but he didn't kid himself; if these Chinese boys wanted to cause trouble then they would. He just hoped that they wouldn't.

Steve was particularly looking forward to a family gathering back home. Rasha had invited a few friends and family to a local Indian for a meal. Anya was coming and so was one of Steve's brothers who he had not seen in years. There were going to be some surprises!

Chapter 20

On arrival back at their London base, Rasha was waiting for him. Steve was pleased that he had taken the opportunity to catch up on some sleep on the coach, as they left hand in hand to return to their love nest. Rasha wanted to tell him all about things at work and more plans for the future.

'Rasha, would you want children? I mean eventually?' Steve asked.

'Why yes, Steve, why do you ask me that now?' she replied intrigued.

'Just wondered. So what are we doing tomorrow?' he asked expecting a pre-arranged itinerary.

'I haven't actually planned anything; you said you don't like me to over organise things,' she said as they stepped off the tube and headed towards the flat.

'Yes, sorry, whatever you like,' Steve replied, trying to sound casual.

'Let's go to bed,' he continued as they walked through the door and into the flat. She nodded.

They collapsed on the bed, undressed sensually and warmly enjoyed each other, caressing, remembering, exploring. They just lay together, enjoying the moment.

'Hey, isn't it that family and friend's meal tonight?' suddenly Steve remembered. 'What time is it?'

A frenzy of activity ensued with irons, makeup, clean shirts and perfume everywhere as they rushed to get ready on time. They burst into the restaurant as the last to arrive to rapturous laughter and applause. Steve hugged his brother - it must have been more than ten years. Mark had said that he just could not face visiting him in that place.

'How's Mum and Dad?' he asked.

'Mum's OK,' he said, 'but Dad is getting to look his age now. You must come to see them soon.'

Steve hadn't seen them since his release. He hadn't had much contact during those ten years, or much before that since joining the army. He didn't feel particularly close anymore, but now was a good time to start again. 'Yes I will,' he replied.

Rasha couldn't help feel a little sad that she had no one there. Anya, Ben and Steve were effectively her only family now. She was so sad that her parents had never met Steve and that she had lost all trace of her family back in Egypt since her escape to Cyprus. The other guests were a few friends they had met along the way. Lance unfortunately couldn't make it. Once things had calmed down and people had got their drinks, they all started to sit down for the meal. They had ordered a mixed Indian banquet in advance to keep things simple.

'Where have you been?' asked one of his mates. 'We checked, you've been back from Scotland for hours!'

'Where do you think, mate? In bed of course!' he said with a smile.

They all laughed and drank and ate. The meal was good, the atmosphere warm and friendly and the wine flowed. They took their time over the meal, getting to know people for the first time or renewing old connections. It was a lovely evening.

After the meal had all but been cleared away Steve turned to his brother and said, 'I think it's about the right time now,' and he went off towards the toilets.

Mark stood up and gained their visitors' attention, including most of the other guests in the popular restaurant. Gently he asked Rasha to come out to him where everyone could see her for a moment.

She felt puzzled, but complied. Mark had asked so politely, she had not met him before but he seemed so nice. Rasha stood by him as people fidgeted and looked towards them.

Steve appeared from a side door and walked slowly towards Rasha and Mark. He took her hand and knelt down before her on both knees. Looking up into her big brown eyes he said, 'Rasha, you are everything to me. I sense that I only came to realise this long after you did and knew that I would. You have stuck by me and sustained me through these difficult years....and now I love you and want to share my life with you Rasha, have children with you and grow old with you. Rasha Jamour, will you marry me?'

Silence turned to tears and applause across the room before Rasha could even compose herself. He waited, and with tears of her own she eased him up from his knees to say 'Yes,' with a loving kiss.

****

Their lives continued to flourish, with Rasha's studies and work and Steve's activities with Lance. Lance's team was really beginning to bond well and Steve was getting less flak as the new boy and beginning to forge a role for himself. He was interested in the media side of what they did and started to write a journal of their events. There had been some press interest and Lance had encouraged him to foster those links. One local paper and an outdoor magazine had shown sufficient interest to want to link up with Steve while they were away, a sort of correspondent role, which he relished.

Rasha and Steve seemed to cope well with the fluid nature of their companionship. Steve's itinerary was always flexible and he usually spent several nights a week away from home. He did still ponder about the risks to Rasha of leaving her on her own, but Lance had tried to help him to put it into perspective; they had been subject to a vague open ended threat and that they couldn't allow it to disable them, so he got on with it. Rasha didn't mention it and he didn't want to raise her anxiety so Steve didn't refer to it either, but he did wonder how much it bothered her.

Plans for the wedding were going well. Given Rasha's separation from her family, the guest list was going to be small. Steve didn't have strong links with his family either. His father was getting infirm and may not wish to travel and he anticipated only one brother, Mark, attending with his partner. Anya was making real efforts to trace anyone with the vaguest connection to Rasha either back in Egypt or here in the UK. She desperately wanted to find someone from her family to share her day with her.

Rasha's studies went well and she qualified in business administration and was offered further promotion in the law firm to head up the support team to one of their offices. This meant more travel, longer hours, but of course more money and as they had never been comfortable financially, this was a bonus, so she accepted. Steve was proud of her. His role with Lance was great fun, but didn't attract a great deal of money, but she encouraged him to follow his dream and maybe the journalism side would offer opportunities in the future, particularly as he got older and if they had children and they wanted to spend more time together. For now however, Rasha was content just to have him in her life, out of prison and to see him thriving.

They settled on a civil ceremony, followed by a modest buffet meal and some entertainment for about 25 guests. There weren't children in the family to act as bridesmaids or pageboys, so the ceremony was kept simple. They decided not to opt for traditional wedding dress and Steve bought a smart suit and Rasha wore a stunning outfit; a smart fitted suit in a pastel apricot colour.

On the day of the wedding the flat was a hive of activity. Sadly Steve's father had died just the week before and his mother was not fit to travel. His brother however was going to make it, although he had split up from his partner and would be on his own. Family representation would therefore be very limited, but in a sense, Lance and his team, Anya, Ben and some of the members of the law firm had effectively become their family. Lance had agreed to act on behalf of the bride's father and to 'give her away' and Anya had managed to track down a cousin who now lived in France who Rasha would remember as a child when they used to play together. Her presence was to be a surprise for Rasha. Even some of Steve's old mates from the army surprised him and had written to wish him well.

The guests were assembled and the bride arrived. The service was personal and dignified without being too formal. For Rasha and Steve it represented triumph over adversity, love sustained, hope and freedom. It was a great day.

The buffet was a success, allowing people to circulate freely and catch up. Rasha had been delighted to be reunited with her cousin and be able to hear some news from home. Lance and the team agreed that it was one of the nicest weddings they had ever attended and one of the most committed partnerships they had ever known.

Mark called for people's attention.

'Hi, everyone. Thank you for coming and sharing this day with us. We are not proposing to prolong this part of the day with long speeches before the dancing, but just wanted to acknowledge your kindness and support for the happy couple.'

There were cheers and laughter.

'Yes, thank you all,' reiterated Steve. 'I am indeed a lucky man. Rasha, thank you for giving my life meaning and for marrying me today. My only wish is to make you happy.'

Rasha then got to her feet and spoke quietly.

'I can't tell you how happy I am. I came to England as a foreigner and had nothing but a man I loved who was in prison. People have been so kind to me and so accepting, this is my home now. Many of you will know the story of how Steve and I first met and how he rescued me from tyranny in that desperate place in Cyprus. I had just landed in the country and was only sixteen. He was my first allotted 'customer' before I was due to be dispatched to Stephan Markou for his personal use alone. When Steve first looked at me however, I knew it was to be different. As he led me through the streets that night to sanctuary with Anya, I knew we would spend our lives together. It was meant to be. Somehow through all the chaos of civil unrest and war we were to meet on neutral territory. How can that be? I have often wondered. Is that what they call God? I don't know.

172

That night as he left me on Anya's doorstep with a peck on the cheek, he left me with his last £20 and a note for Anya. Steve, I never spent that money, and here it is; I will always keep it,' she said, raising her skirt and producing it and the note from her garter.

'The note said that you had found me and had taken me to her because "I believe you can help her". Anya, you too have been my savour. You have been more than a sister to me.

'Steve, I owe you my life and now it is yours, and it is ours to share. I love you, Steve Mantel, and I know I always will.'

With that she raised a glass, kissed him and there were more tears and more applause.

Steve looked up at Lance who too looked emotional and he saw Sandy McGill with his arm round Bob Pearce in a Special Forces hug.

'Bloody hell lad, let me buy you a pint for heaven's sake before I start to cry. I haven't felt so emotional since my first fuck!'

Chapter 21

Steve and the team were due to give a presentation to a leading business development and management recruitment firm in London and Steve was late.

'Where is he, boys?' asked Lance. 'We can't have this. He's in for a serious bollocking when he turns up!'

'Tosser,' said Sandy, 'we'll have to crack on without him. Probably shagging that bird of his!'

'Just coz you'd like to!' gibed Bob.

'OK boys, come on, to work. Bob you'll have to cover Steve's bit on publicity and regular reports,' commanded Lance.

'Yeah, OK Boss,' Bob replied.

****

Steve stepped out of the car to meet B3 and his bodyguards.

'Mr Mantel, a married man now I see. You wouldn't want to lose her would you?' he posed.

'Fuck off!' Steve spat back.

'Come now, Steve, I remind you – you are in no place to negotiate. I did mention that for our protection service we might require payment. Well the time has come. Here's your task...'

B3 went on to describe how he wanted Steve to assassinate a Russian scientist whilst he was visiting London next week. His role was in research into biological warfare and he was suspected of selling information to North Korea. A stronger Korea in the Chinese sphere of influence was not acceptable. They would be suspected however, so B3 had been instructed to find another way, and that way was Steve. He was handed an envelope with further information and £250,000 for expenses. How he did it was up to him but they made it clear that they must receive evidence of his death by the end of the following week. It would be on the international news, but to avoid any uncertainty B3 wanted to receive photographs and his severed little finger from his right hand wearing a distinctive family ring.

'The good news, Steve, is that we only use assassins once. If successful, that will be the end of our contact. If not, you will be dead...and so will she.

'Oh, and by the way...we have something of yours that will only be returned on receipt of what I asked for.' He stepped forward and handed him a photograph of Ben, clearly held in captivity with a copy of yesterday's *Times* held next to his head.

When the blindfold was removed and Steve was released on to the streets clutching his envelope, this time he knew where he was. He headed by tube back to Lance's base, knowing that he had missed the presentation by now.

'Thank you, Gentlemen, for a very interesting presentation. I feel sure our chairman will want to do business with you. We will be in touch.'

As the team left they felt pleased that they had done a good job. Lance was confident that this was going to lead to a very significant contract to train and develop future chief executives and captains of industry in leadership, team work, decision making and planning. They were buzzing.

'Come on, guys, let's get back to base, dump all this stuff and head for the pub,' Joe, one of the Aussie climbers suggested to unanimous approval. They had all quite forgot about Steve, until they burst into their base to find him sitting there looking very sombre.

'Where the fuck have you been?' demanded Sandy. 'You Tosser!'

As Steve explained, the mood changed instantly and the group returned to military mode. The threat was obvious - to the lives of Steve and his family, to part of the team, so in a sense to all of the team. Thoughts of celebration in the pub were immediately forgone, this was serious. They all knew that this moment may come as they cleared the table and examined Steve's information pack.

'Right,' said Bob, who had recent experience of diplomatic protection after leaving the Marines. 'So we have a target. We need to know more about him; Sandy get onto it. Sounds like he's a despicable shit who needs taking out, none of us would lose any sleep about wasting a bastard like this. What are our options? Short notice, urban environment, high profile guy; a shooting would be difficult and we don't want to risk getting caught. We also need a deception plan to deflect suspicion and push blame onto someone else, unfortunately not including the Chinese, so probably the Russians themselves?'

'We need to eliminate the obvious option first, before we go any further,' said Lance coldly. 'Do we share this with the authorities? If we do the risks are obvious. If they know B3's boys will just kill Rasha, Steve and Ben anyway, even if we have wasted the Russian. But we could approach MI5 again? Give them the opportunity to complete the operation?'

'No, I wouldn't trust that slimy MI5 shit as far as I could throw him. They may do nothing, let the Russian live, take the opportunity to discredit B3 and sacrifice Steve, Rasha and Ben. You heard him say that Steve would be expendable. No, I say too risky and too much hassle, and anyway, Lance you know, even if they wanted to intervene, they'll never get clearance to act on this in the time scale,' said Sandy, and Bob nodded. Lance reluctantly agreed.

Steve was bemused, MI5? What? he thought. The two climbers looked at each other bemused. 'Sorry guys, we feel a bit out of it here, we didn't reckon on this sort of stuff. This is your arena!' said Joe.

'Yeah, I don't remember your advert including "experience in assassination would be an advantage"!' replied Brent.

They all laughed and it broke the tension. 'Hey, you alright there fella?' asked Brent, turning to Steve. 'It's your life we're talking about here.'

'And Rasha's and Ben's,' he replied quietly.

'Are we agreed then', asked Lance to them all 'that the risk of going down official channels is too great and that we are prepared, as a team, to launch an independent assassination operation, knowing the consequences for all of us if we get it wrong?'

The pause was too short to measure. Looking round the room the answer was obvious and immediate. Bob and Sandy particularly, despite their ribbing him had really taken to Steve and privately admired his courage, his sense of right and wrong and his unbreakable love for Rasha.

'For a mate Lance, we'd all expect nothing less,' said Sandy, and that was true, so there was no debate. An agreement was set.

Joe and Brent were relieved to be sent to the pub with orders to bring back some beer and fish and chips later while the others started planning. It was going to be along night.

'Right, first thing,' said Lance before the Aussies left, 'we have to have absolute trust on this and absolute silence outside this group, nothing must leak. No one must know that by the end of next week we haven't been away as planned, exercising in Scotland. They all agreed. 'Actually we better warn off our two Ghurkha colleagues that plans might change. They are already setting up in Scotland. I'll put a guard on Rasha all week, Steve, you'd better ring her and say that plans have been brought forward and you won't be home tonight but are going straight to Scotland, OK?'

'Yes, will do, and guys, thank you,' said Steve sincerely.

'No worries mate,' said Joe, as he and Brent left.

When Steve got to ring Rasha he knew her well enough to know that she wasn't too convinced by his cover story. He just hoped that he got away with it. He'd also mentioned that the school had allowed Ben to join them in Scotland and that it would be good experience for him.

The planning team were working through the options, pros and cons with military focus and precision.

'So we are agreed that a shooting in public would be too difficult and too risky. Neither would it quite be Russian style. We could go for a helicopter shooting, that gets over some of those problems and gives a quick escape?' posed Bob.

'Still very risky and could escalate into a bloodbath, and the government could even authorise the RAF to shoot us down. No, I don't think so,' replied Lance. 'How about a kidnapping? We could create a distraction, steal him away unnoticed and kill him somewhere quiet and leave the body somewhere prominent.'

'OK, that's got potential,' added Sandy. 'I'm sure we could do the front end, the second phase is more tricky though; to leave him somewhere prominent risks detection. We have to be really careful here and to ensure sufficient presence on the ground in Scotland to create a bomb proof alibi.'

'Yes, noted. We need to come back to the deception plan,' confirmed Bob.

'Where could we leave him? Perhaps a double bluff and leave him at the Russian embassy, so they can vehemently deny involvement to the point that it will be believed that they killed him.'

The team worked on that idea for an hour or so and decided that access was too prominent and the risks of detection therefore too high. They moved on to consider other places with an obvious Russian connection and a viable plan started to come together.

It was the early hours of Sunday morning. It seemed that Ben had been lifted on Friday and the team had until the following Saturday to complete the operation, provide the evidence and secure Ben's safe return. Then they would need to brief him and ensure that the deception plan was solid and bomb proof.

Their attention turned to Scotland. They decided that it was best to leave the two Ghurkhas, Thapa and Pun to set up the deception plan and to create an illusion of activity; firstly because they were there and secondly because their look was too distinctive to risk on an operation like this, although their skills would have been useful. They also considered a rotation between all members of the team to drive up and make sure that they were seen in the area. For all to be seen in the local pub would be helpful, say the night before departure.

Sandy was now ready to feedback on his research about the target.

'His name is Alexander Zharkov, aged 42, educated in Russia, graduated from Oxford in Biology and later studied back in Russia for a PHD in Bio Chemistry. He has worked for the Russian Government in research, concentrating on the development of biological weapons that can easily be deployed onto the battlefield with minimal difficulty to deliver maximum effect. Also in more specifically targeted systems that could be used in more clandestine operations.

'He arrives in London on Tuesday and is due to fly to Stockholm on Friday to address an international conference, ironically on the threat posed to international peace and security from instability and nuclear proliferation. I have established which hotel he will be staying in and we can anticipate a modest bodyguard presence and some passing police interest. I am not expecting MI5 involvement. I anticipate that the best time to lift him would be Thursday to be able to deliver him on Friday morning in time for the world's press to react over the weekend, while we are notionally travelling back from Scotland.'

'OK,' said Lance, 'that sounds good. On to the detail; the lift, let's consider the options.'

The team carefully thought through various approaches and again worked on the fine details of a plan. Steve was amused; thinking back to TSP in prison, the thinking skills course, the team had just provided a model example.

They decided it was time to call it a day and get a few hours kip. Later on Monday afternoon they went through the whole plan again, questioning every detail and making some minor amendments as they went along. A sticking point at this stage appeared to be the method of despatch.

'We've worked out how we are going to get to the delivery point and to kill him on sight must be silent and leave no obvious first trace of violence. We also, ideally need something that would implicate the Russians. Sandy, can you sort that?' said Lance.

'Yes, Boss, I'll research it, no probs.'

It was Monday afternoon and time was pressing to have a watch in place to trace Alexander Zharkov's movements in time for his arrival on Tuesday. The team considered that he would arrive in London around midday and that they would watch the hotel to assess the security and level of activity while they waited for him to arrive.

Alexander Zharkov landed at Heathrow as part of a trade delegation as planned on Tuesday morning. Despite their country's differences, Mr Zharkov liked England and had fond memories of his time at Oxford. They were met by a modest reception, according to their status and the perceived level of security. The party of five scientists travelled in two diplomatic cars through London. Passing police interest and occasional escort facilitated discreet arrival at their hotel in good time to receive guests and attend a reception lunch held by several government departments concerned with international trade and development and, of course, security. The Prime Minister was keen to develop stronger trade links with Russia and although cautious this included developments broadly in defence procurement. The government was also interested in what might be Russian intentions in the East in general and were also aware of China's concern about any defence contracts, official or otherwise with North Korea. China had been on the brink of invading North Korea several times in the last ten years and relations remained strained. The West, aided by not inconsiderable pressure from China had however managed to limit and contain North Korea's nuclear ambitions, at least officially. The visit was therefore likely to be somewhat stilted and tense.

Bob observed the party arrive and noted the extent of both the British and the party's own security. This was bigger than the team had expected and was undoubtedly going to make their task harder. The team followed their activities during the remainder of Tuesday before leaving them to a formal dinner with some academic research foundation. Wednesday was due to be taken up by high level meetings and various industrial visits before returning to London for a reception hosted by a consortium of interested business groups.

At a distance so not to be recognised, the team kept a passing interest to establish any patterns of security arrangements around the party. So far they all kept together and were always accompanied by at least three large, serious looking security men. Public interest had been minimal with no public protests. Bob was becoming concerned however at several sightings of a man at a distance that he thought looked either vaguely familiar or instinct just told him was with British security in some form, probably MI5. This worried him, he wondered if this was going to prove too difficult and beyond their limited scope. He would need to discuss this with Lance later when they went through their plans for Thursday's lift again tonight. He soon dismissed the thought however.

Wednesday evening's planning meeting was tense. Lance sensed that the whole team were wondering whether they had bitten off more than they could chew; the delegation was bigger than they expected, so was the security presence, and Bob's observations about possible MI5 interest were worrying. Nevertheless they had committed to help Steve, and both Rasha and Ben's lives were at stake. Lance tried to judge the mood and reassure and motivate the team. Steve appeared the least concerned and the most confident. As they went over the details for the third time, they all agreed on its importance and felt more confident about the plan. Bob also reminded them that Zharkov was in their eyes a legitimate target and it was in the wider interest both to eliminate him and to deflect blame away from the Chinese, if the region was to remain relatively stable and China encouraged to play a more active and benign role in world affairs.

Chapter 22

Alexander was talking freely to one of the other delegates as they walked from the hotel through the streets of London towards the Russian embassy, where they were assured that the ambassador would greet them for coffee and talks. It was then that it all happened.

A small explosion sounded some distance away. Sirens rang out, emergency vehicles roared past and police activity came alive. Two minutes later a second explosion sounded, this time nearer, and Alexander started to feel perturbed. This was too close for comfort as Alexander wondered what was happening. They weren't warned of any likely terrorist threat? Was it crime; a bank robbery? A gas explosion? What was it? Then a large smoke bomb went off near them causing panic in the streets. Alexander lost sight of the man he had been talking to and any of the security men. He could barely make out anything. People were screaming and others shouting instructions from all directions. The situation quickly turned to chaos. Suddenly there was a firm grip on his arm and someone just said in Russian, 'Come with me.'

Alexander followed, feeling confident after hearing his own tongue speak out in the confusion, until his confidence waned as the next words he heard were definitely in English. Sandy bundled him into the back of the car and Bob quickly joined them through the other door, securing Mr Zharkov between them.

'What do you want?' he asked calmly as Steve drove away out of the confusion.

'Don't speak,' ordered Sandy.

Steve drove confidently along their prearranged route avoiding all the holdups they would have created via the small explosions, leaving emergency vehicles confused and entrapped. They drove some distance twisting and turning. Sandy had applied a blindfold to Mr Zharkov and pushed him down in the seat out of view. After what they anticipated was long enough to totally disorientate him, they headed back into central London. It was a risk, but the team had reasoned that the authorities would probably assume Zharkov had been stolen away out of the capital, once, that is, that they had established that he was missing, which the team thought could take some time. Detailed searches, particularly at random were highly unlikely to be authorised in the capital, so they reasoned that the property that they had rented for the last week would not attract attention, particularly for one night.

As the approached the rented house, Sandy injected Zharkov with a sedative to subdue his movements and further disorientate him. He would only be required to get out of the car, move into the property and lay down. Then he would be given more sedative until the morning.

As the car arrived, Lance opened the door and the four men quickly entered before Steve returned to park the car as close as possible. Joe and Brent had been sent up to Scotland to continue the pretence of their training and together with Thapa and Pan had been making sure that the local community knew that they were there and that they were buying enough rations for the whole party.

Back at the house, the team were pleased. It had gone well, despite their reservations. Sandy's preset fireworks had caused sufficient confusion without causing any real harm and the smoke bomb had facilitated their attempt to separate Zharkov successfully. Now they just hoped that the news media would go overboard and that B3 would hear of it, before they had to complete part two tomorrow, which would again be tricky.

Zharkov slept in blissful ignorance.

In the corridors of MI5 messages were flying around, questions being asked and heads being scratched.

'What the hell happened here? Didn't we have an interest in this one? Where the fuck is Zharkov now? And who the fuck has taken him?' demanded the duty officer. 'We better have some good answers quickly boys because the boss won't be impressed, not to mention the Minister!'

'He'll be long gone by now or buried so deep we'll never find him. He's a gonna that's for sure and no loss either,' replied one of the officers.

'Yes, in a sense somebody has done our dirty work for us, but we ought to know who and why!'

Lance had been notionally occupying the house for several days. In London it was easy to be invisible. Occupants come and go, neighbours take no interest. The team sat quietly in the house and topped up on rations while guarding their captive. Any attempt to rescue him or steal him seemed extremely unlikely but they had to be prepared. They went over arrangement again and again for tomorrow, then slept in shifts.

Steve's phone rang, 'It's Rasha, Lance, shall I answer it?'

'Yes, be sure to tell her that you are on top of a mountain; blow some wind across the phone, sound cold and tired...' he replied.

'Steve, it's me. What's happening? How are you?' she asked.

'I'm fine, Rasha. What do you mean, what's happening?'

'Steve, I'm not stupid; I'm worried. There's been a strange man following me about and I haven't heard from Ben. Anya has contacted the school and we don't recognise the men that collected him last Friday. Are you really, alright Steve? Is he really with you?' she asked anxiously.

Steve stopped trying to shiver and stopped blowing a gale across the phone. 'She's sussed it Lance. At least that something is happening.'

'OK, Steve, you'll have to fob her off. Tell her something, but nothing about location or of course the target. I'll swop that guy who is meant to be protecting her,' said Lance.

'Honey, look, we are busy. I can't tell you, but it will be alright, you just have to trust me. I'm in Scotland, its freezing. Listen to the wind...and Ben's OK, we've kept him very busy, for the experience. Thapa and Pan have kept him fully occupied all week. He's loving it!'

'Steve, I can't bear this half truth and uncertainty, I just want a normal life...' she said becoming upset.

'You're breaking up, I'll have to go. Love you honey, see you Saturday with loads of minging kit!' and Steve stopped blowing and rang off.

'Did she buy it, Steve?'

'I don't know. I hope so.'

The night passed without incident. The following morning the team prepared to move Zharkov to Moscow Place to keep the pretence of the Russian connection. It would be very public, but also unexpected. They were to dress in disguise. Steve was the designated driver with Sandy and Bob doing the business. The trick was to look relaxed and blend in - second nature to both of them.

Zharkov was groggy but malleable. They walked him quickly to the car as Steve brought it as close as he could. They set off watching for tails, twisting, turning, backtracking and moving through the early morning traffic. It was just past 6am on Friday. Steve drove steadily trying not to attract any attention as Zharkov groaned and moaned as he was pushed down in the back seat. They drove ironically past Wormwood Scrubs.

'One of your previous residences, Steve?' asked Sandy.

'No, I never had the pleasure!' he replied.

They drove on through the traffic in the direction of Notting Hill towards Moscow Place. The radio news confirmed that the authorities were looking for a missing member of a Russian trade delegation whilst speculating on who was responsible for yesterday's disruption in the capital. Chechen rebels seemed to be the favourite culprits. Zharkov was too disorientated and drugged to register the news story. There didn't seem to be any more police traffic than usual, or any obvious security vehicles. Sandy and Bob would know. The team had planned on approaching Moscow Place from the west, stopping quickly to exit from the car with their captive while Steve circled round ready for a fast pick up once the job was done.

'OK, now!' said Bob, as Sandy injected Zharkov's hand before severing his little finger as instructed. Mr Zharkov didn't appear to be in pain but despite remaining sedated didn't look too impressed.

Stopping without attracting undue attention or risk of causing an accident was not going to be easy but their rusty driver was doing OK. Despite not having been behind a wheel for some time, Steve had quickly caught up with the requirements. No vehicles around them looked suspicious as they approached and Steve slowed down. He saw a suitable stop just to pause and pulled over attracting just a few irate looks and blasts of horns. Quickly Bob and Sandy, in standard business dress, got out taking Zharkov with them. Both men were wearing wigs and large hats. They sat with Zharkov on a bench as if just pausing on their way to work.

Quickly, Bob took photographs of Zharkov on the bench with the place name Moscow Place in the shots. Sandy placed Zharkov's hands in front of him for the benefit of the camera then pushed his injured hand into his pocket so no one would notice. He then injected Zharkov for the final time with a lethal dose as Bob stood over them to cover him. They waited tensely for a few moments to make sure that Zharkov was dead, then left him peacefully sitting on the bench as if just watching the morning's passing trade.

They wondered how long it would be until anyone noticed that the man was actually dead.

Bob and Sandy moved efficiently through the crowds towards their pre-arranged pick up point.

'Steady!' said Bob, noticing several policemen standing more or less where they had hoped to be picked up.

'Was it a coincidence?' Both men were sceptical about coincidences in these circumstances. Had they been sussed? How will the lad react, they wondered?

Steve couldn't identify his mates in the crowds but did notice the police interest in the identified pick up point. He slowed down, concentrated on his driving and went past them. He couldn't see any obvious reason why they were there. Sandy and Bob could however.

They simply glanced at each other, nodded and separated, knowing immediately the procedure to revert to the emergency RV, which was back at the rented house. Assuming that hadn't been compromised, Lance would be waiting for them and they'd set off in two separate vehicles for Scotland. The team had decided that radio communication was too risky and that mobile phones were perfectly suitable to communicate if necessary. The car Steve was driving was wired up for easy use of communication by phone with standard voice recognition number dialling. Sandy called Steve and just said 'Meet you back at the house,' and rang off. He and Sandy had separated to minimise the chances of detection if indeed they had been sussed.

Bob emerged from the tube and went into a large department store collecting a carrier bag on his way to the toilet. There he stripped off his coat, wig and hat and emerged looking like himself, wearing a casual jacket, swinging the carrier bag and walking confidently. Back on the street he kindly donated the bag containing the coat and hat to the nearest homeless beggar, having left the wig in the toilet waste bin. He returned to the tube and doubled back before arriving within observation distance of the house.

Sandy had acted similarly, discarding the hat and wig down a railway embankment. They both watched the house from different angles for some ten minutes before Steve drove past slowly and Lance appeared, left the house and got into the car. No police or unusual presence was apparent as the two men approached the car and got in.

'What happened?' asked Lance.

'I couldn't see,' said Steve.

'I'm not sure,' said Bob, 'but I guess two of the officers had just been dropped off where we had planned to be picked up and were listening to their radios with the other two officers. We have to assume that the messages they were receiving related to the discovery of Zharkov's body. So the search is on.'

'I agree,' said Lance, 'so we need to move fast Steve, to the lock up to collect our van with all our kit in it and head off to Scotland as arranged on the two parallel routes. Time is rolling and we need to be in that pub for the celebration as soon as possible.'

'We also have to collect Ben,' Steve reminded them.

'Yes, of course. We'll take both vehicles to the RV in case of trouble, then Sandy and Bob take Ben with you in the van and brief him in detail all the way on the week he's had. Steve and I will carry on in the car and probably get there first to meet Thapa and Pun. Remember the whole conversation in the pub needs to be loud and about nothing else but the camp, the experience and the usual post exercise banter. Steve, time to ring B3 and confirm he's heard the news... You did manage to kill him, didn't you guys?'

****

B3 was pleased with their work. He was satisfied from the photographs Bob had sent him and the news broadcasts that Alexander Zharkov was dead and that initial suspicions lay with the Russians. He was also aware of the Russian Government's concerns that Zharkov had been talking to Chechens as well as the Koreans, and that had been a step too far. When the team arrived at the designated RV there had been no fuss or ceremony. The finger with the ring had been handed over and Ben returned, a little pale and shaken, but OK. B3 had confirmed to Steve that his debt was now cleared and that they would have no further use for him.

In MI5 they couldn't decide who had the greater wish to see the end of Zharkov - the Chinese or the Russians, but knew that neither would miss his passing. Either way they concluded that this was obviously a professional job and best to let sleeping dogs lay. Ministers were secretly pleased whilst expressing great public sadness at the loss of a dear colleague and important trading partner.

The team were under pressure to make the journey in time. Progress had been slow in parts with Friday traffic. They all felt tired but relieved that things had apparently gone well. Ben was OK, Steve was free from B3 and they could get back to their own lives. They also had much of the £250,000 expenses left to sweeten the pill. Tonight was destined to be a good one!

They arrived at last at the pub, with Steve and Lance being first as expected. They ordered drinks, quickly followed by some food. The London element of the team realised that they had not eaten properly since Sunday, nor slept much. Much as if they really had been busy in Scotland.

Lance made a not too flamboyant speech congratulating the team on their performance in Scotland, welcoming Ben to the fold and outlining future plans to make use of all their newly honed skills over the coming months. Ben was prompted into telling several long stories of great conquest and heroism that Sandy and Bob had rehearsed with him on the journey. By the time they left for their base camp, everyone was knackered, but the team was restored and the Scottish trip had been so well faked that they almost began to wonder themselves whether they really had been in London. Just the singing of songs remained before some well deserved sleep, the journey back home and the challenge of convincing all their families that their cover story was bomb proof.

Chapter 23

'Hello love, we're back!' called Steve as he and Ben walked into the flat.

Rasha rushed in from the kitchen with tears in her eyes and hugged Steve so tight, not wanting to let him go.

'Oh, I so missed you!' she cried. 'And I was so worried, until that strange man outside went. Ben, were you alright? Have they worn you out?'

'Yeah, I'm fine Rasha, just tired,' Ben replied limply.

Rasha busied about helping them bring their kit in and started loading up the washing machine, putting the kettle on, asking them what they wanted for tea, what they were doing tomorrow, asking how cold it had been and how they'd managed to drive back, before suddenly collapsing in tears on the settee.

'Steve, I can't cope with this!' she sobbed, striking out at a cushion.

'What's the matter?' he replied sympathetically, taken aback by her reaction.

'Steve, this half-secrecy, this not really knowing what's going on, the strange man, the school pick up,' she sobbed. 'Steve...just tell me it's all alright...that nothing horrible is going to happen...please!'

Steve felt very uncomfortable not really being able to level with her and he knew he couldn't fool her, that she could read his mind. He tried to reassure her but didn't feel he been very convincing, before changing the subject.

Ben came in and started talking about his experiences in Scotland. Rasha was captivated and seemed somewhat reassured. As he told his stories of trekking through the mountains, hanging onto ropes and learning survival skills, they ate their dinner together. The boys were genuinely tired and were soon ready for bed. Steve was looking forward to cuddling up with Rasha, so was happy to call it a day early. As they cuddled, hugged and loved, Steve told her that he believed it was going to be alright and that he loved her; that at least was genuine.

In the morning they were all up early. Steve was diligently sorting out his kit ready for the next time, carefully cleaning and putting away various treasured items in their rightful place. Rasha had taken the day off work in anticipation to help with the sorting out. Steve wanted to pop out to buy a few things and Rasha gave him a small shopping list to buy several items for dinner. Ben went back to Anya's, leaving Steve and Rasha to themselves. Steve diligently tracked down Rasha's list and returned feeling pleased with himself that he had completed his task, and bought her a little special surprise with some of his share from the money from B3. He had found a little jeweller and bought her a very nice silver pendant, which he felt sure she would love. He entered the flat excited only to hear more sobbing coming from within. Rasha was sitting on the settee with some crumpled up papers in her hands, crying and looking angry like he had never seen her before.

'What are these, Steve Mantel?' she cried. 'What are these?'

'What do you mean?' he replied genuinely confused.

'Where were you this week on Tuesday, Wednesday and Thursday?' she demanded.

'You know where we were, all in Scotland!'

'Then why while I'm sorting out your "minging kit" from a hard weeks training in Scotland do I find these McDonald's receipts and tube tickets in your pockets covering the same dates and various venues in central London!' she demanded, throwing the crunched up papers at him and shaking with rage.

'Rasha, Rasha,' Steve said pathetically, trying to hold her hand.

'Don't you Rasha, Rasha me!' she replied indigently, 'you lied to me Steve. *You lied to me!* What were you doing in central London? Is there someone else, is that it, so soon!' and she stood up and starting banging her fists on his chest.

'I can't live like this Steve...if I can't trust you,' she cried, beginning to calm down.

'Just be honest with me...that's all I ask.'

Steve sat in his armchair while she rampaged up and down the room.

'Rasha, I'm sorry, I really am. OK, I've been in a bit of trouble, best you don't know, I can't tell you...but its sorted now...believe me, it's OK. You'll be fine, we'll be fine,' he said firmly.

'Was it to do with that man who threatened you before?' she asked.

'How do you know about that?' he replied instinctively.

'I'm not stupid, Steve; don't treat me as such. I can read you. I knew in the prison when you were down, when you were in trouble, I just knew. I know when things aren't going your way and when you want to protect me. You placed that man to watch me, didn't you? Then I just wonder why. What danger was I in? Who was it that collected Ben from the school? If I can't trust you, if you can't be honest with me, then we have nothing, Steve Mantel, nothing,' she said, now speaking more softly, looking deep into his eyes, deep into his soul.

Steve gulped, he knew that she was right and what she had said was entirely reasonable. He had let down the only woman he had ever loved, the one most important person in his life. Unforgiveable, he thought. How was he going to talk his way out of this one?

'Rasha, I love you, I think I always will. You are the most important thing in my life and I would never want to do anything to hurt you. But you must understand that my life is not straightforward. I'm still a lifer. I don't nor never will work in a comfortable office and come home every evening at five o'clock. I need adventure, excitement. I was denied that for ten years, probably the best ten years of my life, physically at least. Sometimes I will need to keep some things from you in order to protect you. I won't do it lightly and I will try not to deliberately lie to you. This time I did, because I felt I had no choice, and I still think it's best that you don't know why. I can only say that the receipts are genuine, but they were for me, no one else. I'm sorry, but I can only say again that you will need to trust me. Talk to Lance about it, or better still to his wife, she will know what I'm talking about; living with secrecy.'

'But you are not in the army now. You're a civilian, aren't you? I don't know whether what you were doing was part of some state security role, a matter of principal, of justice and courage, or straightforward criminality.'

'Rasha I can't say and I ask you to accept that, but I will tell you this; it was nothing to do with criminality, it was a matter of principal and whilst I'm not looking for it, I can't guarantee that it won't happen again... That's all I can say,' he said as he looked her straight in the eye and held out his hand towards hers.

Rasha looked back at him intensely, and after a few seconds took his hand.

'OK, I can go along with that some of the way, but Steve I want you to promise me that you won't ever put your life in danger, and that you will at least be honest with me when you are being dishonest.'

'Rasha, my life is about danger. I've lived that way since I was sixteen, and what do you mean about honesty?'

'I mean at least tell me if you are engaged in something, so at least I know; that's all I need to know.'

'OK Rasha, I promise you that I won't put my life in danger, recklessly, unnecessarily or needlessly and that I will warn you when things get iffy.'

'OK, "iffy" it is!' she said, pulling him towards her to embrace him strongly.

'Steve, I don't want to argue, I hate it when we do,' she said passionately.

'Well, just do as you're told then!' he replied as she threw a cushion at him, and he smiled. He then remembered his shopping.

'Oh, I did do my shopping for you... And while I was out I bought you this,' and he gently handed her the jewellery box.

She opened it and he had chosen well; he was right, she did love it.

'Oh, Steve, its lovely! It's not been bought with dodgy money has it, Steve?'

'No,' he assured her. 'Try it on.'

Rasha moved into the bedroom to look in the mirror and Steve followed and stood just gazing at her, until she noticed and turned to meet him as they fell onto the bed, kissing, remembering, connecting and reaffirming their bond and their love, whilst the world was about to wake up to a new disaster that again would challenge the international community to act decisively to help the vulnerable.

Chapter 24

The phone rang at 0500. It was Lance.

'Steve, we've had the call out from the UN. We're on. I need you at base ASAP. We're off to Central Asia!'

'OK, thirty minutes,' said Steve, kissing Rasha as he explained, and jumped out of bed. Rasha was pleased for him, but disappointed for her, for them.

Steve scrambled into the bathroom then collected his few bits of kit that weren't already at the base. Excited at the prospect of the unknown, of adventure, of the chance to test his response, he rushed around and was ready. He left with the thought of being alive again, being challenged to the limits of endurance, to be needed, to make a difference.

'Rasha, I truly love you. I promised life wouldn't be dull! Wish me well and I'll tell you what I can...when I can.' He kissed her passionately and left her standing in the hallway alone again. Rasha tried to be excited for him, but she felt empty, lonely and worried. Would this be the time he didn't come back, she thought? This life was really hard.

Sandy burst through the door nearly knocking Bob over.

'Great, guys, what's the form?' he asked with boyish excitement. Steve crashed in after him. The Aussies and the Ghurkhas were already on the road with the climbing kit and a pre packed aircraft box of essentials on the way to Heathrow.

'I've dispatched the others with the kit, but I just wanted to tell you what I know. An ice melt has caused extensive flooding in the mountains of Central Asia. The international community are reacting and the aid agencies, but the obvious first conclusion is that reaching some of these areas is going to be extremely difficult. They were already isolated before this happened, so the UN committee has instigated their emergency plan and contacted us amongst others to be prepared to fly out immediately to be parachuted into the more remote areas to administer immediate relief. It's now 0630, we fly at 0800; is everyone ready?'

'You bet' said Steve.

'Great! Beats a civvy Saturday night out, deciding whether to have one or two pints of warm lager and a packet of crisps or nuts!' said Sandy.

'When we drop in it's going to be tough,' said Lance. 'It's very isolated with high mountains and jungle to fight through before getting to any of the isolated village communities. It could well take us days just to get there.'

'Hey, come on this is what we need; a real challenge. This is what we've trained for and these people really need us right *now*!' said Bob.

They had all pre packed a range of kit for different scenarios, at the UN's expense, so that they were ready to go at very short notice. This would really test their resolve as a team and their respective expertise. There was also a feeling amongst the team members of being jaded by war; the experience of death and destruction at somebody else's command had lost its appeal. This somehow seemed more worthy of their efforts.

Excited, confident and full of expectation they set out to rescue the unreachable communities at risk of imminent starvation, hypothermia and disease and to satisfy the western world's conscience to intervene.

They were quickly processed through the airport procedures and onto the specially chartered plane. They were due to fly to Central Asia, then to board a small aircraft to fly into the drop zone. The flight was tense as ever while the team waited to get out there on the ground. They were all used to the feelings of anxiety; the waiting, wondering, hoping it all goes well. So much can go wrong on the drop zone. They landed and boarded the small plane and were soon in the air again. Ten minutes to the drop zone. The team made final adjustments and exchanged glances before the warning lights came on and they tumbled out into the night sky. All the parachutes opened OK and they began floating down to earth.

On the ground, the team soon organised and gathered their kit and moved off. In many ways this was so much easier than military operations with the risk of immediate action on landing. The only enemy here was the environment; the thick jungle, the climate, the altitude and the rough terrain. No one was shooting at them.

Lance signalled the direction they had been given to the nearest mountain village, some three kilometres away. Lance told Pun to establish coms before they set off, but there was no signal. The ground was steep and wet as they started moving in the hope of finding people in trouble that they could help.

Initially they made good time, but the lack of preparation and familiarity was already beginning to tell as they all struggled to adjust to the alien environment. The heat, the humidity and insects, the water, the exertion and the sheer discomfort all took their toll, but they pressed on. The rate of progress through thick jungle is notoriously slow, but here there were the added difficulties of altitude and steep ground - it was really tough going.

After ten hours of hard physical effort they hadn't covered much distance. Lance nevertheless reckoned that they could reach the first village by the end of the following day. They looked at each other, smiled and persevered through the thick jungle. This was an obvious opportunity for Thapa and Pun, the two ex-Ghurkhas, to come into their own. This was their natural environment. Generations of familiarisation had bred very tough and resilient people, which together with skills passed down from father to son on survival, navigation, outdoor living and basic medical provision created extremely hardy and useful people for just such a job as this. The British Army traditionally only recruited the fittest and strongest from this already elite group, so their two friends had passed all the tests, had some hard military experience and the added motivation of setting out to help their own people. Lance knew that at the end of the day these two men in particular would be crucial to their success or failure and would never falter. They were indeed an inspiration to the whole group, despite their collective experience.

'Well, better than walking through the streets of London, guys?' posed Bob.

'I could do with a kebab,' replied Sandy.

'Thinking of your stomach again?' responded Steve.

'Your stomach just falls out of your arse, doesn't it Sandy?' gibed Bob.

'Yes, usually, but not so far!' responded Sandy not long before he was proved wrong.

'Where's the nearest bar then guys, I'm just ready for a few tubes!' asked Brent, one of the two Aussie climbers.

'Oh, it's just round the corner,' replied Lance, like a father to young children in the car driving to a family holiday.

They pressed on. At times they could see some of the damage caused by the water surge. When ice melts it sets up a combination of problems, not just the resultant thaw and flood but also the rock and mud slide as large pieces break away and gain momentum as they fall.

As the sight of debris and damage became more familiar, the team saw their first body.

'Is that the body of a woman over there?' called Pun.

'Sadly, looks like it,' replied Bob as they picked their way across to check.

As they got closer it was evidently the body of an old woman on her own. Lance reckoned they weren't far now from where they expected to find the village. They trudged on further, carefully picking their way through increasing amounts of flood debris. As they got nearer a pitiful picture started to emerge. Houses were smashed, people killed and a general scene of devastation awaited them as they approached what used to be a small habitation. After checking around, the team found no one alive. The power and force of the surge looked to be so great that nothing could have survived. The smell of death was in the air. Thapa and Pun took the lead in saying a few prayers and trying to record something of what they found. The team sat down, exhausted and gutted. This was not what they hoped or expected to find. They put a brew on and took the opportunity to cook some food. They were all more than ready for some sustenance.

Lance tried to work through their options in his mind. Sadly they had trudged through the most difficult of terrain for hours, all carrying extensive supplies of emergency kit only to find that no one in their allotted target area had survived. This was so disappointing. For Thapa and Pun it was more personal than that; these were their people and they had all been lost, brushed aside by the power of nature in an instant. They were just gone. Lance had to acknowledge that he hadn't been given much of a brief beyond this point.

'Guys, if we gather round, let's just consider our options,' he said quietly.

'My initial brief, I have to say, was pretty vague at this point. We had hoped to be able to spend several days here and make a real difference, but that clearly is not the situation we find ourselves in.'

'You mean that's it! There's no plan B?' exclaimed Joe, the other Aussie climber.

'Pretty much,' acknowledged Lance. 'Come to think of it, instructions for evacuation were pretty vague too,' he added. Lance had to confess that he had rather assumed, like the military, that this operation would have full back up and a range of contingency plans, but he was starting to think that he had been way too optimistic for what resources the UN had to offer. After all the emotion of last week, this operation had offered a real and timely chance to move on, a chance they all felt that they needed, so despite their collective experience, they had gone with the moment and now things were not as they had expected. They were half way up a serious mountain in a very isolated and remote area of Central Asia, with at the moment, no coms and no back up. This wasn't good.

'Seriously, guys, we could easily be facing our own survival situation here very quickly,' interjected Sandy sombrely.

'Sandy's right,' responded Lance. 'I reckon we make camp around here, see if we can get a signal to report back what we've found and seek further instructions on any alternative realistic target we could aim for from here, otherwise it's all been a waste of fucking time and effort!'

'Sounds sensible,' agreed Sandy. 'Come on, Steve, let's find a place to set up and get sorted before dark.'

Steve and Sandy set about establishing a cooking shelter and erecting tents, while Joe looked for a supply of clean drinking water and Brent gathered some fire wood. Thapa looked around in dismay before sitting next to Lance.

'Colonel, given the size and power of this slide, I fear the chances of anyone surviving here are minimal, so our chances of finding a settlement that needs our help are equally remote. In which case Sir, all we may be able to achieve is to extract ourselves safely.'

****

Rasha was eating at Anya's with her and Ben this evening. He had not gone on the disaster relief mission as he had an appointment for army selection that week. As they sat and talked and wondered how the team were getting on, the news came on the television.

'Concern mounts in the international community for the plight of the people of Central Asia in the light of the recent ice melt and consequential natural disaster. UN attempts at providing relief have been severely hampered by bad weather and damage to the areas infrastructure. So far there are no reports of relief getting through into the vast interior since the disaster happened three days ago.'

The report continued as they stopped to listen more intently. After the UN Secretary General made a statement and contact details were given for donations to the disaster relief fund, there was a pause.

'Casualties are already estimated to be likely to be in the thousands as bodies are starting to be recovered in the less remote areas. Concern is also mounting for a team of experienced British rescue workers who parachuted in two days ago and have not been heard of since. A UN spokesman said yesterday that "It is unusual not to have established radio communication with this group, but they are all very experienced men, mostly ex-military who are all well equipped. Efforts to trace them will continue along side our efforts to bring relief to these desperate and needy people".

'A representative from Oxfam acknowledged earlier today that timing was becoming critical. If relief could not reach people soon, then sadly casualty figures would inevitably raise.'

Ben wished he was out there with them. His mother was glad that he was not, and Rasha looked extremely worried.

Chapter 25

By the following morning the weather had closed in and conditions were bleak. Any realistic thoughts of rescuing anyone else would need to be put on hold. Pun had got out of his tent to check around the camp that everything was OK. He opened the front zip and popped his head into Lance's tent to find him up and dressed.

'Colonel, the camp is secure but visibility is down to virtually zero and I'm afraid the radio equipment is no good, Sir.'

'Great, the weather's shit and the radios fucked!' came his crisp, if not accurate reply.

'I had a good look at the UN radio last night Colonel, and I don't know when it was used last but I doubt that this kit had any realistic chance of working before we left,' said Pun quietly but with the convincing tone of experience.

'Um,' responded Lance, deep in thought, 'what now? Pun, gather the team together would you, and please it's not Colonel or Sir anymore, it's Lance on this trip, OK?'

'Yes, Sir!' replied Pun immediately, and scurried off to raise the troops.

'Colonel wants us all for briefing now!' he cried into each tent firmly.

When all were gathered, Pun turned smartly to Lance, although they were all sitting down and was almost about to salute when Sandy jumped on him to stop him.

'We're all civvies now Pun, you daft sod!' he exclaimed.

Lance paused whilst they all laughed. 'OK, guys; to say we are seriously in the shit is probably to understate our position, so listen in! Between us I reckon we probably have about another three days food each, which could spin out for six or even nine days if necessary. Fresh water is limited, but we can sterilise it or boil it. Has anyone had the shits yet?' he enquired.

Only Sandy replied to be met with more laughter.

'We have plenty of suitable survival kit, so on the face of it whilst we are here on our Jack Jones with no back up and no reassurance that anyone will know where we are with any accuracy, no one is shooting at us and we can survive. The challenge however is how to get out, because we won't survive indefinitely. If we are where we think we are at the identified target location we could easily be ten days walking away from any chance of evacuation. With Thapa and Pun, I'm sure we could manage that if we have to, but we don't have maps of this whole area and it would be tight, too tight if anything else went wrong on the way.'

Thapa confidently reminded them that tigers also roam freely in the area.

'So what are you suggesting Lance, apart from beam me up Scotty or phone a friend?' asked Sandy to more raucous laughter.

'Hey, that might be a point,' said Bob, 'the radio's knackered but did anyone bring a mobile phone up here?'

'I did!' said Steve.

'Thank God we have a youngster along!' gibed Sandy.

'I don't suppose you brought any lager too, did you?' asked Brent more in hope than expectation.

After more laughter, they had realised that Steve's state of the art phone, although no doubt on limited battery strength in the cold, could at least leave a detectable signal that would confirm both their position and that they were still alive. High on the side of a bare arsed mountain, miles from home, sitting in a damp tent being rattled by a severe gale, Steve switched on his phone and attempted to ring Rasha. After 30 minutes of sporadic attempts the battery was dead and he wasn't sure if he had registered a connection or not.

'Well, it was worth trying; let's just hope it worked,' said Bob.

'OK, guys, we've done technology, now I think it back to basics. If we stay here and eat all the food in the hope of being rescued we'll probably all die, so my vote is to get off our arse's whilst it's light and move down the mountain as best we can and try to maintain the hope of helping any poor bugger we might find on the way,' said Sandy.

They all looked at each other and agreed that was the best plan, indeed the only plan available. Whilst Lance sat with Thapa and made the best attempt they could at a serviceable sketch map and charted a general direction, the others went about packing up camp. Within an hour they were all fed, watered, packed and ready to go. The weather had eased a little giving some visibility, but progress over this difficult terrain was going to be slow, if it was to be safe.

As they set off, Joe turned to Brent and said, 'Aren't we usually on a beach somewhere at this time, mate?'

'Yes, but this year I booked this instead!'

'Fair enough!'

****

Rasha's phone registered a message. She looked at her monitor and knew it must be Steve trying to get through. She quickly pressed locate and it give her a sheet and grid reference in Central Asia, a time and altitude. He was alive!

'Anya, Anya it's a message from Steve; he's OK, well at least he's alive!'

Anya hugged her as Ben came in and heard the good news.

'Rasha, best let the UN know,' suggested Anya.

'How can I do that?' she asked.

'Didn't they leave a contact point of any kind?'

'Not exactly, I can't just the ring the UN Secretary General, can I?'

They laughed. 'I suppose if I rang the Para Depot, they'd help,' Rasha suggested.

'Or the BBC?' suggested Ben.

Several phone calls later and the message was passed and registered.

Miles away from the mountain, at least Rasha, Anya and Ben were relieved.

Chapter 26

The team picked their way across the broken ground and the picture of devastation continued all around them. When water in all its forms moves on this scale its destructive power is enormous. Moving water, ice and debris are not discerning, they take the shortest route down, regardless of what may be in its path. Trees, homes, whatever won't hold it and people out in the open have no chance. It also meant of course that any paths or tracks that did exist that would have eased their passage and helped with navigation were no longer there. It remained slow and really tough going.

As they emerged out of what probably was a strip of forest, the remnants of a village appeared around them, with several bodies and parts of bodies cast amongst the debris. It was a horrible sight even for such hardened ex-soldiers and adventurers. Nature it seemed could surpass even man's awesome ability to wreak havoc and destruction.

Lance could feel the pain on Thapa and Pun's faces. The others, too, were clearly moved by the experience. Then in the wind Bob thought he heard a cry.

'Stop!' he shouted. 'Listen...was that a human cry?'

They all paused, and with military discipline despite the cold, the wet and the exhaustion, listened intently to Bob's invitation.

Through the gusts and turbulence of the wind Thapa could also hear a faint cry. It sounded like a child. He called to the others and they moved across to where he indicated. As Joe approached the sound it was becoming clear that it came from behind a cliff edge.

Sandy approached cautiously, conscious of the unstable nature of the ground. 'Be really careful everybody; the ground could just slip away from us at any time,' he warned.

Brent got down on all fours and crawled the last ten metres or so very carefully to reach a large boulder, reasoning that it offered some stability.

'Use the rope,' ordered Lance. Joe quickly started unpacking kit while Brent shouted back that he thought he could hear a child's voice, but couldn't see anybody. Lance called him back to use the kit they had all expended so much energy lugging for the past few days. Joe and Brent put on their climbing harnesses and started preparations to abseil down the mountain to get a better view. Bob and Sandy glanced at each other expressing unspoken concern about the wisdom of risking going over the edge in such circumstances. Nevertheless, the team agreed to proceed. It would have been inconceivable for Thapa and Pun to have not attempted a rescue with or without a rope. The key point was finding a suitable bomb proof point to tie onto. Joe scoured the ground very carefully before selecting the two best available belay points.

Confidently the two climbers prepared to move as safely as possible. Brent elected to go down the rope, with Joe providing support at the top. The ground was horribly wet and slippery, but Brent was very sure footed. The experienced climber moved with expert precision down the unstable mountain slope, abseiling on one rope and attached to another. The others watched on, there wasn't a lot they could do to help. Thapa and Pun moved to a dip alongside Bob, put a brew on and starting cooking some food. Lunch, dinner, whatever, time didn't really register, it was still daylight and at that point, that was all that mattered.

After a few tense moments Brent arrived safely on the first discernible shelf and looked over into the abyss. He found that he was on an overhang looking down at a drop of easily 2,000 metres. The cloud had cleared and he had a good view of the ground and open space in front of him. Bob moved some twenty metres to the side to get a good angle and a view of what was happening in relative safety.

'What can you see Brent?' cried Joe.

It was difficult to communicate in the wind but voices carried on the gusts. Brent lay down as far as he could on the wet shelf and peered out. Some one hundred metres below was another small shelf and there he was pretty sure he could see a tiny body that appeared to be moving.

'I can see him, boys!' he shouted back up. Bob confirmed from his view point that Brent was indicating a second shelf some way down.

'What's after the second shelf Bob?' cried out Lance.

'Nothing, Lance. Nothing! Just open space,' he replied.

Joe could anticipate the next move of a further abseil down the mountain. Sure enough he felt Brent's weight on the safety rope. Brent moved off over the edge and out of sight. He easily moved down the abseil rope across firm hard rock to where the child was laying. As he approached it became obvious that the poor kid was in a bad way. He shouted 'OK' on arrival and the rope went slack. The others waited in eager anticipation.

The child was conscious but obviously dehydrated, cold and in pain. Quickly Brent unpacked some more kit, this wasn't the time for first aid; Sandy could handle that back at the top. He just needed to evacuate the casualty. Efficiently he unrolled a small emergency stretcher and some slings and wrapped the child securely and tied the bundle on. The next part was going to be tricky. Brent needed to free climb up and over the overhang to be able to signal to Joe to retrieve the safety rope with the child in tow. Then he would need to guide the load over the rock before Joe could fairly easily pull the load back up to the surface leaving Brent to tie onto the remaining abseil rope and with Joe's help climb back up. Bob was still in position but couldn't see beyond the first shelf, but had a pretty good idea what Brent was likely to be attempting. Helpless, he just wished him luck.

Carefully Brent started his climb up and over the unforgiving rock overhang. This part of the mountain at least was firm and the rock hard and in good condition. Brent chucked to himself; this was the sort of climbing he lived for! He was in isolation with risk and daring; a free climb with nothing between him and the abyss. On a better day he would have been in his element, but today he was wet, cold and hungry and the priority was not challenge or recreation, but rescue. There was a child's life at stake.

With fingers straining, reach at his maximum, Brent picked his way up the rock. The wind whistled round him, but wasn't too bad right up against the rock face. He persevered and pulled himself up and over the top, back into Bob's view onto the first shelf.

'He's made it back to the first shelf!' shouted Bob, his message being greeted by the others with admiration.

Brent hand signalled and pulled twice on the safety rope to alert Joe to start pulling up the casualty. Although the child was small in stature and light in weight, this was a delicate move. Carefully Joe pulled up the rope. Brent guided it safely past the overhang and up towards the top.

Sandy waited, ready to receive the casualty. As the small parcel arrived, spirits lifted and Joe took hold of the child and handed him to Sandy. Sandy scurried away, back to the dip with the others and started work. The child was in fact a little girl, probably about six or seven years old. Sandy quickly gave her a warm drink, checked her over for obvious injuries and wrapped her in warm clothing that Thapa had placed by the cooking fire. Sandy couldn't see any obvious damage, but assumed there would be broken bones and possible internal injuries. It was hard to tell, but after a while the child smiled. Pun was able to offer a few words of comfort that the child seemed to understand. They all felt a huge sense of relief and pride at having brought her back from beyond the cliff edge to safety. They all acknowledged Brent's efforts and skill. This, after all, was what they had set out to do. Pun held the child firm in his arms and started to spoon feed her some hot broth when suddenly a terrible sound broke the calm and their celebration.

They looked up to see the ground moving. A whole section of earth along a gully starting some hundred metres behind them had started to shift and to creek and to slide down towards the cliff edge. It was moving past their position which seemed to be firm, but looking up, Joe, his two massive rock delay points and the climbing rope attached to Brent were all clearly sliding and gathering pace.

Lance and Steve had positioned themselves on the opposite side to the others to gain a second vantage point. They too were in a hollow, protected from the wind and could only watch with horror as a large strip of ground between them and Bob's group was sliding towards the cliff edge, gaining momentum and filling the air with the powerful sound of a mud slide grinding through soft ground.

As both teams watched helplessly the slide gained momentum and took Joe closer towards the edge as his feet began to get coiled up in the spare rope. Suddenly Thapa broke cover from the far side and sprinted across to Joe in an attempt to help his desperate efforts to release himself from the rope quickly enough, but it was too late. As Thapa reached him they both hurtled over the edge together with the two boulders way out past the first shelf and into the empty space beyond. As the rope tightened Brent was projected into thin air following them in a trail of debris, dust and water.

All went silent.

In an instant, the team had lost three valued members and friends, all gone into the abyss. They all knew that there was no chance of survival for any of the three men.

The camp fell very subdued as they all decided as a mark of respect as well as a practicality that they would pitch camp in this area for the night. Lance and Bob carefully surveyed the ground for any signs of weakness or movement and settled on what they perceived to be the safest place to make camp. Pun cradled the child, who having eaten had fallen asleep in his arms.

Chapter 27

It was an uncomfortable night. With the wind raging and thoughts of their lost mates, no one slept very much. In the morning everyone was very subdued. It was a really hard and a low point in their time together. The two Aussies had added something different to the group. Neither came from a military background and the others, whilst at first sceptical, had come to find them refreshing. Thapa had been such a solid and reliable member of the team. Ever generous, warm hearted and so determined. Pun particularly found his loss almost unbearable. That first dull, damp, cold, wet morning just added to their sense of sadness.

Bob and Sandy remained stoic, glanced at each other occasionally and just stuck to the task. After a meagre breakfast almost in silence, it was left to Lance to try to raise morale.

'OK, guys, I share your sadness, but we have to be focused here, for the child's sake if nothing else, if we don't we risk total failure. We could all die here.'

The others knew that he was right.

'We have to move on today and we still have a long way to cover. Sandy, can you oversee the redistribution of kit. We will need to leave some stuff behind now. Keep any personal items from our three mates obviously but otherwise select what you think we will need, what we can carry and ditch the rest. Steve, can you help Pun rationalise the food, I know it's hard but at least this takes away the pressure of potential hunger, then you must return to writing your journal. There will be a story to tell here. We must remember our mates and the sacrifice they have made and the best way to honour them is for us to succeed... Sandy, you will of course need to check the girl over, too. Bob, you and I will examine the options for the rest of the route. Pun, please give us your opinion on the route when you have finished with Steve. OK, guys, it's time to move forward.'

It had to be said and Lance had struck the right tone. Some momentum returned and with it, of course, some dark humour.

'Hey Sandy, be sure to save any of Joe and Brent's nappies for the child!' called Bob.

'Steve, you can change your sleeping bag now, you keep saying the one you got was crap!'

Lance smiled and moved away, giving the guys some space. The route options they decided were largely going to be dictated by the state of damage on the ground. They anticipated that they could well find further settlements on the way down. The state of the ground would set the pace, any tracks would be a real bonus but if they were left to plough through virgin territory or flood damaged ground, it could prove to be a very slow process. Pun agreed and reported back that food supplies now looked OK. Sandy was happy with the kit and the little girl was awake and talking. They were ready to move off. Pun volunteered to carry the child to be able to reassure her as they went. Whilst talking she was still very weak and her degree of injury remained unknown.

As they headed off, all were tired and jaded but tried to stay positive for each other. Bob strode off with Lance and shared some thoughts about home and the future, then thought back to London.

'Lance do you think there will be any comebacks from the Zharkov incident?'

'No, I don't think so. I think we played that one just right. All the indications would lead the authorities to look elsewhere. Nothing would realistically point to a small independent operation like ours.'

'I hope you are right.'

Looking out in front of them the weather was beginning to clear and they could see for some distance the ground stretching out in front. Their general bearing was hopefully going to take them in the direction of the largest settlement in the area, from where evacuation was realistic. Depending on the ground, however, they agreed that they could still be several days or longer away from their destination.

The next three days were just pure slog. Slog through debris, fallen trees, uneven ground, poor weather and poor visibility. Pun cradled the little girl all the way, fed her, talked to her and tried to keep her calm. He said that she spoke in riddles much of the time, but occasionally described snippets of what had happened. In trying to make some sense of it Pun gleaned that her village worked in either forestry or tourism, serving the more adventurous in providing local knowledge, guides and assistance in carrying equipment and supporting expeditions. Local people had been concerned about the weather, the unusual level of rain fall and the risk of landslides. Details of the actual disaster were far more sketchy, just glimpses of the panic, loss, pain and confusion. The poor kid didn't seem to remember any details about her family or even her own name. Every evening with care, Pun and Sandy tried to identify any injuries and to treat her as best as they could. Pun was getting attached and Sandy was getting concerned.

On the fourth morning the weather had improved overnight and Lance and Bob were able to sit on a rock and observe the valley below and to get a greater picture of where they were and the best route down. Locked in their own little world cut off from everyone else the team had no idea of the mounting concern for their safety back home. The UN had at last, after much pressure from Anya woken up to the fact that a team working on their behalf was effectively unaccounted for, if not lost, in a hostile environment. Other teams were by now working in the low level areas, but any attempts at reaching more isolated communities had been abandoned in the belief that no one could have survived this long without assistance. It had taken Anya to very firmly advise a senior UN official face to face of the potential negative impact of any adverse publicity should the team not return. Only then it seemed did any momentum grow to even start to look out for them, let alone search for them. Anya and Rasha kept up the pressure whilst privately they both had faith in the resilience of these guys to survive in such circumstances. As the days went on, however, with no communication, they were starting to fear the worst.

Looking at the full vista from their rocky position Lance and Bob were pleased to be able to make more sense of their progress. It seemed as though they had managed to travel over several high valleys in the last few days and now sat on a front facing slope overlooking some form of settlement in the bottom of the next valley. They were reasonably confident that the thrust of the landslide had travelled to the right side of them, hence missing the settlement, and that paths and trails were still in existence over on their left side. Therefore it made sense to move left and take that route down the valley. They called over the others to share their thinking and take into account their views. They all agreed that Lance's suggestion was the best plan.

'Given the complex borders and politics in this area of the world, are we sure which country we will emerge into and hopefully evacuate out of?' posed Sandy.

'Um, Sandy's got a point there. Pun, as we get nearer, would you be able to tell?' replied Bob.

After further discussion they agreed that language in this part of the world could vary valley to valley and jurisdiction didn't count for much, as long as wherever it was they were looking at was at least on board with the UN attempt at disaster relief. In any event there was not much enthusiasm for any alternative, so they decided to press on. Given the improved going they reckoned they were about two to three days away from the settlement.

'Is our little friend going to last that long Pun?' asked Lance.

'Yes, Sir, of course,' was the crisp reply. Sandy didn't look so confident.

As they set off again the mood had lifted with the prospect of being closer to evacuation. By now, given the difficulties they had faced, all the members of the team were suffering with something. Old injuries, fresh blisters on previous blisters, nagging knees and ankles and, of course, stomach upsets were all taking their toll. Other than the environment however, as they all kept reminding themselves, nobody was actively trying to kill them. Apart from perhaps the tigers, but they hadn't encountered any of those.

The team made good progress and reckoned as they stopped overnight that they could reach the settlement by the end of the following day. Food supplies by now were pretty meagre, although fresh water was becoming readily available from mountain streams. Sandy proudly returned to camp having had a crap, with some quarry in his hand, having managed to kill an animal. No one was quite sure what kind of animal it was, a sort of rabbit like creature, but it certainly tasted good cooked on their fire that evening.

In the morning exuberance was tempered with caution as they set off for what they hoped would be their final leg of the journey. Sandy couldn't help but chuckle to Bob as they trekked down the mountain side.

'This is when we suddenly get surrounded, captured, stripped and taken away for two days torture before escaping into the evasion part of the operation, isn't it?'

'No, not this time Sandy, this is pussy really!' Bob replied.

For the first time, Steve allowed himself to believe they would definitely survive, and he was so looking forward to seeing Rasha again. He had missed her terribly, not just because of the hardship, but because he was now sure that she was the centre of his world, a world which he was unaware was about to change dramatically.

By mid afternoon they could clearly see activity in the community below. It looked like major works were underway to restore roadways, and at one point Lance was pretty sure that he saw the distinctive blue helmets of UN troops. Pun was still not entirely sure, however, which country they were about to encounter.

Bob was winding Steve up by reminding him that he hadn't been in touch with his probation officer as regularly as he should have.

'See those UN troops down there, Steve? They've been sent to arrest you for breach of licence!' he taunted.

'Yes, it's back to the slammer for you!' added Sandy for good measure. Since the advent of electronic reporting, complying with the requirements of licence had become less restrictive. Verifiable reporting by phone or computer had become common place and allowed for more flexibility to accommodate travel and work. Nevertheless, Steve knew that they were right and that he would need to report in as soon as possible. Craig, his probation officer was aware of the nature of their task and the likely difficulties of access to reliable communications, but he accepted that Steve would have reliable witnesses with him to verify his movements if need be.

By late afternoon they were in striking distance and Pun could detect several different mountain dialects being spoken at once. Then suddenly through the trees a group of men appeared and approached them. Sandy felt suspicious and immediately went to firm his grip on his weapon, only to be reminded that he was unarmed. As he moved off the track and into cover as a precaution, Pun came running past straight towards the group to be welcomed like family. After a while of surreal hugging and loud chatter with the others just looking on in confusion, Pun returned to reassure them that the village was friendly, they knew of the teams existence and were pleased to see them all alive. Also there was a plane that would be made available to fly all eight of them out. They obviously were not aware of the loss of Thapa, Joe and Brent. Pun was able to explain what had happened and the welcoming committee seemed genuinely saddened by the news.

They walked the last short leg together with Steve joining in with Sandy and Bob's banter and Lance walking quietly alone at the back.

'Hey, mines a big Mac with double fries and extra relish, and you're buying big boy!' gibed Sandy to Bob.

'And you're buying the first ten pints, son!' came the reply, 'Hey Steve they may have a brothel here, too - you have experience of those places don't you!'

'Fuck off!'

Lance wondered quietly to himself whether this really was the life for him now, or was he past it? Had he been effectively given notice to quit? He wasn't sure about that but was certain that he would never commit to a UN operation like this again. He had learnt a bitter lesson that this was not the army he was used to. The operation by its nature had been set up at very short notice, but the lack of clear planning and any back up arrangements had surprised and severely disappointed him. It could and indeed in three cases had been fatal.

On arrival in the village Pun was relieved and clearly proud to untie the child from his back and lay down his human bundle in front of the local people. They looked on in amazement and admiration at the possibility that a child could survive so long in these circumstances. As Pun recovered his bundle however, it became evident that she had lost the struggle. Somewhere along that route since he last checked, the child had silently slipped away. Pun was gutted, but the local people were still both grateful and inspired by both the little girl's determination and the team's efforts to save her.

After that there was no enthusiasm for the big burger or the ten pints, although the choice in any event was somewhat limited. After a short conversation between Lance and the local UN commander the team were spirited away and onto a cargo plane that evening, without so much as a cup of tea. After a short period of prayers was said for their lost colleagues and for the child, they were gone.

As they reflected on the whole affair sitting in the back of the tatty old cargo plane that had definitely seen better days, the team wondered whether it had all been worth it. Pun was quiet. Steve was quite a little despondent. All were very tired. Bob and Sandy had their quiet moments then would look at each other and one would fart or scratch his bollocks or something to start them laughing again, but for Steve, somehow this time that was not enough. Lance was used to the loneliness of military command and although their structures were much looser than that, he could only draw on that previous experience.

'So they all died for nothing,' said Steve in both sadness and anger.

'No, they didn't,' retorted Sandy quietly and firmly. 'The two Aussies knew the risks. They were both very experienced climbers and offered their expertise in the service of others. Thapa was brave, which was admirable and foolhardy in equal measure, but again it was his love for others that drove him to try to save Joe.'

'But after all that the child died,' said Steve, starting to feel bitter and emotional.

'Yes, but we didn't know that at the time; all we could do was give her the best possible chance.'

'But there should have been others who we could have rescued!'

'Steve, it doesn't work like that, those people weren't there for our benefit. Yes, it would have been more satisfying and less messy if we had found whole settlements still alive, but the fact was that we didn't, probably simply because they were no longer there.'

'So how do you live with that?'

'Steve, I've lost mates in action, seen people die who shouldn't have died and yes, I've killed a few, but do I dwell on it? No, I move on. I've taken part in some excellent operations, well planned, well led and well executed, but I've also seen my fair share of fuck ups and there will always be fuck ups, that's human nature. So don't punish yourself, take

236

your head out of your arse and look forward, because that's all there is.'

Bob and Lance both offered Steve a reassuring glance as the old plane lumbered through the isolated and difficult terrain towards a British military base and a shower, food, a comfortable night's sleep and transport home.

Chapter 28

There was a warm welcome at the military base. The staff had been warned to expect them and had made a special effort to accommodate their needs. It had been an uncomfortable journey overnight with only fleeting opportunities for sleep. On arrival in the early hours the team were treated to a full English breakfast and after a shower and change of clothes had a few more hours comfortable sleep before a full debrief. Then they were given access to the medical team if required and an opportunity to contact home. Bob was first on the phone and was immediately distracted by a family problem while Steve and Sandy sorted through the team's kit ready for departure. Pun was trying to arrange a flight direct to Nepal.to see his family, whilst Lance was continuing to register his displeasure about the whole affair and make sure that the families of those who had died were properly informed and supported. Sandy had carefully packed the personal items from each man that they had managed to save to send on to their families.

When Bob came off the phone, it was Steve's turn to phone home.

'Sorted Bob?' he asked.

'Yes sorted!' he replied.

When Steve got through Rasha sounded so relieved. He did think that it must have been very difficult for her with no idea of how they were other than his one message which confirmed their location and existence earlier, but it wasn't that which concentrated his attention.

When Steve burst into the room the others weren't sure what to think by the look on his face.

'She's pregnant! Rasha's pregnant!' he shouted out.

As one, Bob and Sandy replied, 'is it yours, son? You're never there! How's that happened?'

'Piss off!'

'Don't they cut your bollocks off in prison and feed them to the dogs?' responded Sandy.

'No? Prisons have gone soft Sandy,' replied Bob.

'Oh, well maybe it is then? Fancy that!'

'Steve that's great news, congratulations!' said Lance adding some decorum.

'Sorry Steve, of course that's fantastic,' said Bob, realising that he needed to respond a little more sensitively.

They pondered on timing and names and whether he'd be a back or a forward and so on, until Bob and Sandy had decided that the new arrival would best be called Piece Mantel and captain England at No8. Lance did try to remind them that their speculation may be a little premature, but to no avail as this good news refreshed their spirits and lifted moral all the way to the bar. Lance was a gin and tonic man and unusually for a Ghurkha, Pun could more than hold his own where drinking was concerned. They wasted no time in 'wetting the baby's head', conducted a full drunken christening with several hymns and danced the conga into the soldier's dining room for fish, chips and mushy peas before returning to the bar until the small hours.

****

Return home was a far more sober affair with the reality that there was not much to distract them from the gutting conclusion that their enthusiastic and admirable attempt at humanitarian rescue had failed. Lance felt particularly responsible and disappointed. Pun did get his flight to Nepal so would be away from any recriminations and both Bob and Sandy brushed it off as one of those fuck ups, and that fuck ups happen.

The impact on Steve was more lasting, however. He became quite despondent. He was delighted by the news of Rasha's pregnancy and at the prospect of being a father, but was starting to experience feelings of self doubt and anxiety as the euphoria of release had passed and life on the outside wasn't proving to be that easy. Trying to balance the demands of a relationship that had been effectively suspended for ten years and to get established in a new career was harder than he had expected.

The team decided that it was probably a good idea to take a break at this point and then actively recruit and look to re-form as a viable unit. They felt it was too early to seek to replace their lost colleagues so soon and maybe some time apart would be healthy. On a more practical level further advance bookings for Lance's services were somewhat limited at that time. Lance had other commitments to keep him occupied and Bob and Sandy both returned to private security work for a while, which left Steve a little out on a limb. With too much time to ponder he was starting to drift into heavy drinking and gambling to fill the gap.

Steve continued to do some work with Lance. Whilst he did write up his report for the UN, it didn't launch him into a career in journalism as perhaps somewhat unrealistically he had hoped. He did write articles for local papers sometimes, but it was very spasmodic and unreliable as a source of income.

Rasha's pregnancy proceeded well without incident but she was worried about Steve. He had become more distant and would sit in silence, seemingly staring into emptiness. Rasha had spent some time with Lance's wife while the team were away and had gleaned some insight into the types of difficulties that often occurred for service families and those effected by extreme stress. On Anya's advice she did try to talk to him about accessing help but was rebuffed forthrightly, so tried a different tack and asked Lance to approach him about it. Craig too had noticed a difference in

Steve's mood and motivation and was also ready to express concern.

Fortunately, Steve did start to listen and to draw on some of the lessons from his prison experience in dealing with emotions and applying positive thinking. He discussed obsession with Craig and reflected back how Sandy was apparently such a survivor, he didn't dwell on things, think too deeply about them and moved on rapidly leaving shit behind, when shit happened. Lance reminded him that although it was now some twelve years ago his experiences in Afghanistan could still haunt him and putting that together with his experience of being imprisoned and the disappointment of the Asian adventure was enough to shake the foundations of the most solid and stable characters. In other words he encouraged him not to be too hard on himself and whilst work was quiet to enjoy his time with Rasha. All of these things helped him to refocus on what was important to him and not to become obsessive about failure and disappointment.

Rasha encouraged him to give more time to assisting the Lake District mountain rescue teams, which he did successfully, gaining their respect. This led to a break; to cover a mountain marathon event for a local newspaper. His reporting was well received and it helped restore his confidence.

An opportunity arose to run some adventure training for an international school in the Far East and Lance encouraged Steve to apply. He was successful and spent six months working abroad on the project and sending regular reports and articles to a variety of publications, returning just in time to be there for Rasha at the birth of their twin daughters, Joy and Hope.

Ben was approaching his finals of his degree and had secured a place to train at Sandhurst as an army officer. He still hoped to join the Parachute Regiment, which remained very much in existence as the MOD ran into heavy opposition to its plans to amalgamate elite forces. The logic of shifting resources away from heavy tanks and artillery into greater priority for infantry however, had finally been accepted to meet the perceived need for flexible forces capable of rapid deployment. Advances in technology also allowed for significant reductions in the number of Royal Signals troops and again reassignment to infantry. There was even talk of limited reinstatement of some old amalgamated regiments under these plans to increase the number of infantry battalions. The Mercian Regiment, for example, was proposed as a model with it remaining the organisational hub supporting two battalions each of Staffords, Cheshires and Worcester Sherwood Foresters. The potential return of the distinctive Staffordshire knot cap badge was a very welcome development for many in army circles, particularly in Staffordshire.

Rasha took to motherhood superbly and the girls thrived. For Rasha and Steve this was a very happy time in cementing their relationship and in starting the journey of family life. Both Anya and

Ben were very supportive and actively involved in helping the new parents.

Then a significant break came. Lance was aware of a scheme between the army and the press to promote the role of war correspondents and to set up a training school. In winning the publicity war and keeping the public on board there was widespread cross party support for this venture. Steve readily applied and was successful. His break into journalism coupled with danger and adventure had come at last.

PART THREE

Chapter 29

The Military School of Journalism was established at the Royal Military Academy Sandhurst. Steve Mantel had been a private soldier who never thought that he would enter this establishment in any capacity, let alone as a student with officer status. It was a proud moment. Added to which, during his time there Ben was also due to start his military training, and whilst there would be very little time to socialise they would have some contact and a sense of mutual support.

So Private Mantel became Mr Mantel. The MOD had taken some persuasion to accept him on the course given his history and that he remained a life sentence prisoner on licence, but Lance with the support of the probation service had managed to persuade them that this was both reasonable and justified. The MOD reasoned in any event it was unlikely to attract any negative publicity as there would be some restrictions on Steve and he would not be thrown into the limelight. Key factors in winning the argument had been: identified work on risk reduction had been completed, no emergence of new risks or concerns about manifestations of previously identified concerns, good work reports from a variety of settings and cooperation with licence albeit mostly via electronic reporting. All of which made a viable case for an application in principal to suspend supervision in the future after completion of a suitable minimum time on licence. Apart from these technicalities the MOD were also swayed by the fact that Stephan Markou had by now been thoroughly discredited.

Steve settled in and soon was enjoying the course. He found the other candidates interesting and was surprised by the depth and variety of experience within the group. Course input included some basic military familiarisation as not all the candidates by any means had previous military experience, nor had it been a pre requisite. Lectures on world affairs and politics followed with some fascinating presentations from some of the existing big names in the field, who between them had covered most of the conflicts abroad involving British troops within the last twenty years. The group worked on journalistic ethics and presentation style both on camera and in writing. Although Steve had studied hard whilst in prison he felt that he came from very humble origins in South Shields and lacked some of the experience and education of many of the other candidates. Most were graduates, several with degrees in English from some of the top universities. Steve had never considered himself to be an academic, far from it, but what he lacked in education and intellect he felt he more than made up for in experience of war, adventure and hardship. He did wonder how some of the more academic types would cope with the harsh realities and discomfort of war.

There was also some useful input on dealing with stress, some attempt to offer understanding of the pressure on service personnel and how these factors might impact on a war correspondent. Interestingly the next phase of the training was to involve outdoor living and survival skills with exercises in reporting likely scenarios using all forms of media communication. Steve was looking forward to this phase and hoping that he could excel.

Only a small number of the directing staff were privy to information about Steve's background. He was however prepared to share his experiences with others, and some of the group members remembered his case in the media at the time. His circumstances did however warrant close scrutiny, and Craig, his probation officer, was regularly in touch and in receipt of progress reports. Agreement had been reached in advance that any serious emerging doubts about his suitability would quickly result in dismissal from the course. In the event no such concerns emerged, indeed Steve did very well and was one of the more successful candidates. Discretion nevertheless ensured that he was not considered for the best student prize in order to avoid publicity.

Steve was reassured to hear from Ben, who seemed to be doing alright on his officer training course. Steve also had regular contact with Rasha and spent most weekends at home. The twins were growing fast, developing and keeping Rasha busy. Steve felt so proud of her in the way she coped with it all so well. Lance constantly reminded him how lucky he was and what a wonderful wife Rasha was.

By the end of the course only a small number of candidates had seen it through to the end and were passed and approved to apply for jobs in the field. Steve was well organised and had sent cold applications to all the major newspaper groups in advance. By the time the course was completed there were only very limited adverts for this specialised field at the time, so he was delighted to receive a reply from one of his early applications. It was from a major newspaper group who were looking to send two more correspondents to Japan to report on the story of increasing tensions on the Chinese/Japanese border. Several violent clashes had already occurred and a good deal of diplomatic posturing was being exchanged as the world watched in fear of the potential implications if this dispute were to escalate.

'Good morning, Mr Mantel. We are so pleased that you could respond to our invitation prior to normal adverts going out,' said the man from the newspaper who had met him at the door and was about to show him round. 'We understand that you are amongst the first graduates from our new Military School of Journalism and are looking for a position in this field of work?'

Steve went on to explain his background and experience. The interviewer seemed to be impressed with his outdoor credentials but seemed surprised that he did not speak at least several different languages. No ability to communicate in either Japanese or Chinese looked like it was going to be an obstacle. After further questions and a tour of the building, Steve was set a written test whilst his host went to confer. After lunch Steve was called back to face too different members of the newspaper staff, a hardy looking older man who impressed like he'd been out there and done it himself and a very personable, smartly dressed young woman who evidently had not.

'Mr Mantel, Steve, can I call you Steve?' said the older man, whilst Steve nodded, not used to such polite consideration.

'Can I be straight with you?'

'Yes, please do.'

'We are impressed with your spirit, your initiative and your breadth of outdoor experience, all of which I feel sure would stand you in good stead for the rigours of this type of work. My concerns however are twofold; your relative lack of journalistic experience and the questions that inevitably arise about your self control in stressful situations, given your history. Neither, incidentally, do you competently speak a range of foreign languages.'

Steve at least appreciated the straightforward approach and they talked openly about the issues that he had raised and Steve tried to reassure them.

'Yes, I can see that. You're right, I don't speak other languages - I can't do other than simply acknowledge that. My experience of journalism is also what it is, as I've honestly outlined in my letter to you. As regards stress and self control however, I can give you plenty of examples of positive behaviour in the light of provocation and challenging circumstances, and as I'm sure you can imagine, it wasn't easy persuading the MOD to allow me access to this course,' Steve responded.

The two newspaper colleagues nodded sympathetically. The young woman asked a few more HR type questions and outlined their standard conditions of service.

'Right, I'll tell you what I'm going to do here, son. I like your honesty, your hunger for this work and your attitude. We can teach you the rest. I'm prepared to take a punt on you, Steve, but I have to warn you that any poor or inappropriate behaviour or any actions that would bring the newspaper into disrepute, I simply can't tolerate and would have to fire you. The Japan project is a non starter, but I would like to place you in the team in North Africa where circumstances are still unsettled and attempts at democratic change still fragile. If you can accept that, then we have a deal,' the older man said firmly, extending out his hand.

Steve shook it strongly and accepted whilst telling them about his grandmother, Anya and his wife Rasha and their connections with North Africa.

'OK, Steve, well that's a good start; it gives you some insight and understanding about that part of the world. We'll need to give you some general induction training and site specific stuff on history, culture and language in that particular area. Then we'll fly you out pronto. Does that sound OK?'

The young woman just confirmed details of the package they were offering and that was it.

Steve got straight on the phone to tell Rasha, who was so pleased and particularly excited about the North African aspect. She felt that would make the inevitable separation to come more tolerable.

The induction arrangements proved straightforward and both Rasha and Anya helped him with the background knowledge and cultural stuff. Steve was re energised to be active and to get going again. Given their level of separation, in some ways it did seem odd to impose further voluntary isolation on each other, but they were prepared to work with it. As Steve had fairly warned Rasha, he was never going to be a nine to five man.

****

As he left the flat for the airport and kissed the family goodbye, Steve enjoyed the feeling of mild anxiety that the unknown brings and the return of a sense of adventure. This was going to be a very different challenge, one which he felt utterly ready for.

Chapter 30

Steve landed in the former Libya. After the Arab spring of around 2012 instability and chaos had continued in the region for almost ten years. Now, however, the beginnings of pan Arab cooperation were showing some fruit across North Africa under the alliance of democratic parties committed to sustaining the liberalisation of the revolutions by steady incremental change. Borders had become pretty fluid and large numbers of people had been killed or displaced. What the aid agencies were trying to do, assisted in places by the UN, was to offer safe passage and safe havens for people to regroup, receive food and medical attention before hopefully returning to their home areas. It was to one such camp that Steve had been allocated to work with the relief effort and report back his findings. That sounded straightforward enough, but in reality the politics of aid made things much more complicated. Aid agencies depend largely on donations and those good citizens making the donations want to hear good news stories about the effectiveness of their money being well spent. So a dynamic is created where in order to both survive and further their interests the agencies themselves have a direct incentive to over emphasise success and suppress stories of failure. Steve found himself under constant pressure to feed the media good news stories, not just slightly embellished but at times pure fantasy. It made him unpopular with the agency when he refused to play ball and continued to report what he saw openly and honestly, with what he hoped was a sense of integrity. Several times he submitted honest reports only to see colleagues work get published and they therefore get paid by telling a far more upbeat version of reality. This angered him. What was journalism meant to be about if not the truth he argued, often to blank and completely disbelieving faces?

'Is this man for real?' he heard them say. 'Where did they get him from?'

However, Steve was not to be distracted. He reported what he saw and what he saw could be ugly. He saw a mixture of hope and depravity, of triumph over adversity and despair, of light and of darkness. Individual people's stories touched him and took him back to memories of hearing his grandmother's stories as a child. It was sad, he reflected, that so little had changed; the people who make the decisions are not the people who suffer the consequences; the poor, the sick and the vulnerable suffer the greatest hardships and in large measure the world looks on and does nothing. Yet amongst all this destruction, there was still dignity, there was still joy and there was still life, in places where you would least expect it, and it restored the spirit and faith, whatever that is.

Steve felt it was the right place for him to be helping when he could and challenging the outside world to look, to listen, to feel and to respond. That he felt was of true value and if the newspapers didn't like it then so be it and so what? In his brief phone calls home, Rasha and Anya expressed such pride in and support for what he was doing. Rasha assured him that the girls were fine and sent him lots of love.

Steve was prepared to take risks that most of the other journalists wouldn't in order to seek out and report the truth. He had upset officials, been threatened with death several times and had to fight his way out of situations at least once that he was admitting to. Nevertheless he stuck stoically to his task: to seek and report the truth.

By the end of his brief tour, Steve felt very tired, but proud of what he had been able to do. When he left, even some of his worst critics sought him out to shake his hand and wish him well. On return, the seasoned older man who had interviewed him welcomed Steve at the airport before he went public, just to remind him to be careful for his own safety and what he said to who, but also added that he had heard excellent reports of his work and that personally he was very pleased with him. That endorsement meant a lot to Steve, for the man had taken a risk with him and he was pleased that it appeared to have paid off.

After the brief airport formalities Steve emerged through the barrier to two cold, tired and tearful little girls and a radiant wife. They embraced with all the renewed passion of separation and talked about family, news, the world and nappies all the way home.

****

Steve was able to spend a few weeks at home with Rasha and the girls. He enjoyed the chance to support Rasha and to just be together. He hadn't appreciated just how much hard work looking after twins could be, which only went to increase his respect and love for her even more. Anya and Ben were also very helpful and he made sure he thanked them for their support.

The girls were growing fast, and Steve was fascinated by their progress. This was an aspect of life totally denied him during those years in prison and he was keen to make best use of the time. Anya offered to baby sit one evening which gave him the chance to take Rasha out, to spoil her and to be just a couple again. Those moments were special, knowing that soon he would be back in a danger zone somewhere in the world. As well as family talk, it was good to hear Rasha talk about her job and how well she had been doing before she had the girls. She planned to go back part time when she could. Rasha told him about Anya's work and her links with Oxfam, Amnesty International and Liberty and that she had been invited to speak at an international conference soon on developments in law relating to human rights.

Rasha was tired, but pleased to be out alone.

'I love these times together Steve,' she whispered over the candlelit restaurant table.

'Yes, so do I. Being away so much makes time together even more precious, don't you think?' he replied.

Rasha wasn't so sure but placated whatever implied sense of guilt he was feeling. 'Do you think to the future Steve?' she asked.

'In what way?'

'Well, where we will be, what we will be doing in ten, fifteen and twenty years time?'

'Blimey, no, not really, not in any detail, other than we'll be together. I suppose at some stage it would be nice to have more time together and perhaps to move out of London. Certainly the flat is too small now.'

'Yes, that sort of thing,' she replied leaning in closer, 'that would be nice.'

Steve knew that look and responded sincerely, holding her hand. 'Rasha, if you are asking me do I ever have any doubts, or do I always see our future together, if you are looking for reassurance, Rasha I have never been so sure about anything! Rasha Mantel, I love you and I want to spend my whole life with you and nothing, nothing is going to distract me from that.'

Rasha looked up with her big brown eyes and started to cry. 'I know Steve, I've always known, it's not that, it's...'

'Go on, say it,' he encouraged her as the tears flowed stronger.

'It's...Steve...it's that I worry about you; all this dangerous activity. I worry that one day I will get a visit and that you won't be coming back...Steve, I love you too much to lose you,' she said holding his hand so tightly.

Steve just held her hand and looked into her eyes; he was quite taken aback. He thought what best to say, paused and responded, 'Rasha, this is my life, it is dangerous, but I'm not reckless. I do want to come home each time. Yes, there may come a point when I think it's time to change tack, but please understand, not yet, not for a while. I'm making a difference and there's so much more to do. Please try to understand.'

'It's not that I don't understand, Steve, and I accept it, but it doesn't stop me worrying. Promise me you'll be careful, especially now we have the girls.'

'I will,' he said, as she stopped crying.

One of the restaurant staff came over towards them and approached the table. 'Are you alright Madame, you seem to be upset? Can I offer you a complementary drink at all?'

The interruption broke the intensity of the moment and they both laughed out loud. They looked around to see that others were obviously concerned too, to see that things were alright. They had been so locked into each other that they'd almost forgotten that there were in public.

'It's alright,' she said, addressing the rest of the room, 'we're just in love and sometimes that's really difficult! Yes, thank you, a drink would be helpful.'

'Champagne, Madame ? Sir ?'

'Yes please, make that a bottle!' Steve replied to relief all round and laughter and nods of understanding from the other dining couples.

They finished their meal on a lighter tone and enjoyed the rest of the champagne. Before they left Rasha again apologised to the other diners and again they made gestures of understanding whilst Steve paid the bill and thanked the staff for an excellent meal. They walked the short distance back to the flat, hand in hand.

Standing by the front door as Rasha rummaged through her bag for the key, Steve said, 'I've had a lovely evening, Miss, can I see you again?

As Rasha invited him in for coffee they laughed and fell into the flat to find the twins curled up on the sofa with Anya, all fast asleep.

'Shall we leave them?' asked Rasha as they knowingly looked into each other's eyes and took the rare opportunity to sneak away for love-making given the recent distractions and demands of young children.

As they lay in each other's arms, they felt like they could take on the world. Rasha remembered what Lance's wife had told her; that if you take on a man like this you have to accept a certain amount of separation and disruption, but at least life will never be boring.

Chapter 31

The time to return to work came round all too quickly. Steve had been given an assignment in Iran. It was dangerous. After the first Iran war, coalition troops had remained in the country, much like after similar episodes in Iraq and Afghanistan. The level of fighting had calmed down but nevertheless he had been selected as the most able and suitable candidate to deal with the rigours of the posting and to be attached to 1 Staffords. Steve was delighted both as he was aware what a professional outfit The Staffords were, but also that in the event Ben had not been found suitable for parachute operations and had been posted to the same regiment. Ben had got through Sandhurst fine, but then discovered that he hadn't really got a head for heights and that therefore jumping out of aircraft was not going to be on. The Staffords had been delighted to pick up such a fit and able young officer and he had settled in well before finding himself almost immediately being posted to Iran.

In many ways this was both the best and the worst start to a military career. To go straight into action was what it was all about really, but with such little preparation it risked disaster. There was no time for quant old traditions involving the induction of new officers, or for much male bonding. At least Ben was posted to a Platoon with an experienced Platoon Sergeant, who could guide him, and fortunately Ben was wise enough to listen.

Steve relished his new role and felt comfortable back in a military setting. The troops readily accepted him and he was able to send back reports reflecting some of the realities, but also some touching human interest stories. Marriage proposals on facebook, the birth of children, couples in uniform; there was plenty of scope. He warmed to the generous hearted mixture of Stokies and Brummies he encountered, with The Staffords traditional recruiting area being across Staffordshire and the West Midlands.

Steve was given time to build up confidence and familiarity before being placed too close to the sharp end. The MOD had become sensitive to the plight of journalists at this time after the high profile loss of several well known figures who had been killed 'in action'. It had been decided therefore to bolster up the war correspondents' security by the use of private bodyguards. Steve was due to meet his protector today. At which point who should walk in but no less than Sandy McGill!

'Fucking 'ell', said Sandy as the two men shook hands warmly, 'when they told me I was to look after some journalist nerd, I did wonder!'

'Great to see you again, Sandy!'

'You two obviously know each other so no introductions are necessary!' commented the officer who had brought Sandy across to meet him.

As the two men caught up on news they learnt that they were soon to be deployed into more hostile situations. After several patrols they quickly established a routine. The troops liked Steve anyway, but the addition of an ex-SAS Sergeant gave them a certain edge and helped boost their confidence.

****

It had been another hot day. After checking on a forward position they tramped towards the helicopter pick up point. Steve was in the groove and Sandy was more than happy to take the money for a stroll in the sunshine. The patrol had been routine and uneventful, until they came under fire.

A few rounds whizzed through the air as the patrol looked for cover in what could be a bare arsed environment. There was an irrigation ditch however, and they went for it. As they crunched into the ditch with its less than welcoming dirty watery bottom, the patrol commander Sergeant Potter radioed for help.

'Come on boys!' Ben shouted as the order came through to deploy his Immediate Response Team. The guys efficiently deployed into the helicopter and were air bound very quickly. Ben had never entirely got over his aversion to heights, but he found helicopter flight tolerable. Both the pilot and the team knew the target drop off point and so unfortunately did the enemy. They had used the same position, albeit from very limited options, too many times. This time the reception committee were ready and waiting. It was a trap. Fire had opened up on the incoming patrol who took cover in an irrigation ditch. Knowing the likely tactics the enemy fighters had prepared a series of good positions overlooking the pick up/drop off point in an area of orange trees. They could hear the predicted helicopter approach and saw it slow into a hover and descend down to the DOP. A Platoon of troops emerged from the back in the usual formation and deployed facing the wrong way covering their own patrol. As the helicopter took off the enemy fighter's commander was tempted to try to shoot it down but decided that was a target for another day. Before the IRT troops could establish radio communication with their mates on the ground, the rebels opened up on them from their right flank.

Ben quickly had to assess the situation and remembering what Steve had taught him as a child quickly invoked the mantra: enemy, ground, courses, plan! The enemy appeared to be dug in beyond the orange trees some two hundred metres to his right. It was difficult to assess how many of them, but fire so far had been from small arms only, not from machine guns. His mates from the original patrol, judging from a protruding radio antenna were just off to his left, safely in a ditch. It was actually within shouting distance, which made low tech coms effective. Steve could recognise Ben's voice. Options: to attack or to defend, then regroup and evacuate. There was only one option for a new mustard keen Platoon Commander in those circumstances and his Company Commander had made it clear that Brigade were seeking to regain the initiative against these types of attacks, which were becoming too common. So attack it was going to be. They needed to wheel right and get some cover from the scrub before the trees, then left flanking looked like the better option with greater cover, while a fire group could move up on the right. Also the original patrol could provide additional support by joining the assault group by crawling along their ditch under cover. There, that was the plan.

Ben quickly and efficiently delivered his battle orders and the Platoon moved into well practiced action. The enemy had stopped firing at this point. It wasn't unusual, Ben had been told, for troops to come under these types of attacks and respond only to find the enemy had long since buggered off by the time they reached their fire positions. Nevertheless, he was keen for action and dispatched Two and Three Sections off to the right to provide covering fire and moved himself with his Platoon HQ and One Section skirmishing forward towards the scrub. There was still no enemy fire...

As they approached the scrub, however, Ben's group came under small arms fire from a trench much closer than they had anticipated. He was in trouble. On hearing the fire Sandy took a look from the ditch with Steve by his side.

'We could be in the shit here ,Steve!' said Sandy passing him an automatic weapon from the signals operator who had broken his shoulder getting into the ditch and was in no position to fire.

'I'm press, Sandy, remember, non combatant!' he said.

'Fuck that, Steve, you'll bleed like the rest of us; now use this weapon.'

Looking forward, One Section had managed to move across to a small mound that provided some cover, but Ben's group were dangerously exposed. Sandy was just thinking that they may have to go in at that point, when covering fire from One Section kicked in allowing Ben to move forward. More enemy fire then responded from a further position deeper into the trees and was obviously going for Ben.

Rasha was firmly in his mind, but it was Ben who was under fire, there was no time and there was no choice, this was personal. Steve fired a burst to suppress the enemy fire coming from the trench, then climbed out of the ditch and continued firing as he attempted to assault the second firing point. Ben could hear both the rounds coming dangerously close to him from his front moving towards him from the left and the friendly fire from behind him on his right. He took to ground to see Steve, now dangerously exposed moving forward. He was moving between One Section and the second enemy position leaving them in difficulty to provide covering fire. Similarly for the rest of Ben's HQ group close behind him, their fields of fire were obscured by their own Commander and Steve. Fire then opened up from back right across the position towards Steve. Ben looked up as Steve dropped like a stone.

Sandy fired a grenade from his grenade launcher, accurately and efficiently into the left trench that Steve had attacked, taking it out. Ben's group had neutralised the first and closest trench. Ben had tossed a hand grenade into it with devastating effect. Then Two and Three Sections opened up from the right flank and quickly suppressed the third back right trench, allowing Ben to regain control and move round fast from the left together with the original patrol. They paused, with Ben talking to his Section Commanders on the radio before assaulting the position from the left, sweeping across and taking out the remaining back right trench.

Ben then ordered the Platoon to reorganise around him and consolidate their position. In the heat of the adrenalin filled moment, Ben's excitement at securing the position had taken over. It was left to Sandy to remind him that they needed to go back and recover Steve's body. As the Platoon secured the position, redistributed ammunition and prepared to rebuff any unlikely counter attack, sombrely Ben and Sandy moved back across the ground they had just covered looking for Steve. Ben was pretty sure where he had seen him go down. As they approached, they heard a cry from somewhere to their front and found that Steve had fallen down an old trench and landed on a stinking, rotting corpse from a previous engagement and had twisted his ankle, but he was alive! . . .

On return to the base they were all greeted like heroes. Six rebel fighters had been killed with no friendly casualties! The CO and the Brigadier were delighted with their swift and aggressive response and felt confident that it would send out a clear message. It also enhanced the already excellent record of a fine old British regiment.

The rest of the tour was relatively quiet. The Brigadier was proved right that the earlier actions did seem to have sent out a message that had been heard; don't mess with 1 Staffords!

Steve's ankle recovered, as did the signaller's shoulder, before they all started to shift their focus to their forthcoming return home.

****

Rasha and Anya approached the airport to meet the returning troops with the twins asleep in their double buggy. It was 4am and pitch black. Rasha paused to tie a shoe lace and asked Anya to push the chair. As if from nowhere a car appeared being driven erratically and was approaching them at high speed. It mounted the pavement avoiding Anya and the children but hit Rasha square on from the front and pressed her into the railway bridge behind her. Anya froze, knowing this was not going to be good. The girls woke for a moment then went back off to sleep as their mother lay trapped and dying against a lonely wet railway wall.

Anya phoned the emergency services. She was merely a hundred metres from the entrance to the airport and ten minutes away from greeting Ben and Steve off the plane. She breathed deeply, knowing instinctively that Rasha was in serious trouble and moved forward with dignity towards the airport as the sirens sounded in the distance. She pushed the young, innocent, sleeping children through the airport door, longing for the arms of her two much loved men. As Steve came through the barrier he saw her and knew something was wrong as their eyes met.

'Steve, I'm so sorry, I'm really, really sorry...' she said.

'Anya, where's Rasha? What's happened?' he replied in desperation.

'Steve, it's Rasha...she...she's just been run over Steve...by a drunk driver...' Anya explained through her sobs.

'Where is she, where's the driver?' replied Steve. 'Where is he? I'll tear him from limb to limb!'

'Steve, it was just outside...' And he was gone.

'Go with him,' ordered Sandy to Ben, who ran after him.

Outside, Steve followed the sound and lights of emergency vehicles. He approached the scene and pushed past two police officers to face the shattered car and the shaken driver. Steve punched him hard in the centre of his face, shattering his nose and blackening his eye. He grabbed him by the collar and pulled him out of the car slamming him hard against the roof and shouted, 'You stupid, stupid fucking bastard! That's my wife you've just run over and the mother of our children!'

'I'll stop him, Sarg,' said the young police officer.

'No, give him a few seconds. I'd want that, wouldn't you?' said the wizened old Sergeant as he held the officer back. Steve hit him again.

'You fucking piece of shit! All this because you can't handle your fucking beer!' he said, throwing him roughly to the floor as the officers took hold of his arm.

'OK, Sir, that's enough now; move away.'

'Where's my wife?' he asked distraught.

'She's in the back of the ambulance, Sir, but I must warn you, it's not a pretty sight.'

'I'm used to that, believe me, I've just come from a war zone!' Steve replied.

'But this is your wife, Sir.'

As the sun came up and shone across the roof of the ambulance Steve sat and held Rasha's hand as Ben looked on, and they both could see that her life was ebbing away and she was dying leaving his life was in tatters...again.

'No, no! Steve cried, 'Not my Rasha, not my precious Rasha, no...no...!'

THE END

Epilogue

Steve did recover from the loss of Rasha for the sake of the girls.

The police officers attending Rasha's death recorded seeing nothing untoward and the driver reported having received all his injuries in the crash.

The driver responsible for Rasha's death was eventually convicted of reckless driving only and was sentenced to just two years imprisonment. His defence counsel had successfully argued that as the two women were dark-skinned and it was 4 o'clock in the morning and they were wearing dark clothes, that they and the pushchair should have been lit up in some way to enable his client to have seen them.

Finally the Ministry of Justice agreed to suspend Steve's licence supervision arrangements, endorsing his feeling of finally being out of the shadow of the bayonet. Between them Steve and Anya continued their quest for truth and justice and honoured the memory of Rasha Mantel as a truly remarkable woman.

COMING SOON from Chris Boult

A victim's story:

LOOK FORWARD   The Recovery...

Chapter 1

'We've found her; seems OK,' said the police officer
with a mixture of excitement and relief. 'She's back
in the underground car park from where she was
abducted. She looks dazed and upset, but
physically alright as far as I can see.'

'Excellent! Well done!' replied the operational
commander. I'll let the parents know immediately...
I don't suppose there's any sign of the perpetrator
or any obvious evidence or leads?'

'No, Sir, nothing obvious. Looks like he's just
brought her back and dumped her. I just hope he
hasn't caused any harm in the meantime.'

'Quite. Time will tell.'

****

Unfortunately, in another place at about the same time, events were not going to turn out so well...